Lilac
in
Black and White

CHRISTINE DORAN

ISBN-10: 1533645175

ISBN-13:978-1533645173

For all of you

GLOSSARY FOR U.S. READERS

Most British or Irish books are altered for the American market, to use words Americans understand. I thought it would be nicer to leave the words as they are and provide a short glossary instead. If you meet an unfamiliar term in the book, it might be in this list.

back/front garden	back/front yard
bin	trash can
biscuits	cookies
bunk off	to leave school without permission
chips	french fries
cinema	movie theater
crisps	potato chips (and similar snacks)
dungarees	overalls
football	soccer
fringe	bangs
give out to	scold, tell off
Golden Pages	Yellow Pages (phone directory for businesses)
Guards or Gardaí	Irish police force
Inter Cert	exam taken by Irish schoolchildren at age 15; was replaced by Junior Cert in 1989
ISPCA	Irish Society for the Prevention of Cruelty to Animals
jumper	sweater
junior infants	the first year of elementary school, for age 4 or 5
knickers	underwear (female)
lead	leash
letterbox	mailbox

loo	toilet
maths	math
mitch	see above at 'bunk off'
nail varnish	nail polish
newsagent's	small convenience-type store that sells newspapers, candy, etc.
pantomime	Christmas stage show for children, with songs and audience participation, usually based on a fairytale
pants	underwear (male and female)
plaits	braids
plaster	band aid
post	mail
postman	mailman
pound shop	dollar store
power cut	blackout, power outage
pudding	dessert
queue up	line up
rubber	eraser
runners	sneakers, tennis shoes
school tour	field trip
senior infants	the second year of elementary school, for age 5 or 6
sledge	sled
solicitor	lawyer
sweets	candy
torch	flashlight
wellies	wellington boots, rain boots

CHAPTER 1

January 1986

Once upon a time, a little girl grew up in a tall, narrow house by the sea, with a father who painted pictures and a mother who wrote books, and a big dog who jumped up and down all day. The girl had fat yellow curls that tangled into a thicket every night in bed, and pink cheeks, and big solemn eyes that looked out at the world. Her name was Lilac.

From her bedroom window, Lilac would look down towards the small grey waves bumping up against the pebbles, or the giant white breakers crashing down on the pebbles, and decide what sort of day it was going to be. Then she would choose her stripy tights and her polka-dot dress, or her worn-soft jeans and the orange woolly jumper Granny had knitted her, and go down for breakfast. Today was a jeans morning, though not too wild.

'Let the dog in, would you, darling?' asked her mother.

'Put the kettle on there, Lilac,' said her father.

Lilac stood on tiptoe to reach the bread-bin, and put two slices in the toaster. She flicked the switch on the kettle and opened the door where Guzzler was whining and scratching in the blustery winter morning. The sun considered coming out, but thought better of it and set up camp behind a solid bank of cloud. Guzzler the hound bounded inside, leapt his muddy front paws onto everyone's laps, and then buried his nose decidedly in his breakfast.

'Damn dog,' said Lilac's father through a mouthful of muesli. 'Should be trained.'

'And I just washed this', said her mother calmly, brushing off her knees with one hand and readjusting the newspaper with the other.

Lilac buttered and jammed her toast, and made the two slices into a sandwich. With her free hand, she pulled on a fuzzy pink-and-red hat askance, and then shrugged herself into her warm jacket with the duffel buttons. Guzzler made a beeline for his lead, Lilac snapped it onto his collar, and, munching a goodbye in the general direction of the kitchen behind her, she left the house, in tow of dog.

The wind was brisk but not icy, as an Irish late-January wind should be, and left-over autumn leaves were muddy underfoot as she tromped towards the sea path and off up the hill that curved an encircling arm around one side of the long stony beach. There were dangerous cliffs farther up, but so long as you stayed well back from the fence, you couldn't be blown over.

Lilac was small for her nine years, but she knew where she was going, and looked it. You wouldn't have called her defenceless, even without the large dog loping at her side.

One of Guzzler's grandparents had been a Great Dane, and though the others had clearly been smaller – and maybe cleverer – dogs, he had what Lilac's father described as an overly generous paw-size to brain-size ratio.

A conversation was raging inside Lilac's head, as a small quick voice fought against a deeper, slower one.

– *Margery hates me, ever since the first day she's hated me for no reason. She's just a witch with a b.*

– Don't say that.

– *I didn't say it. And she is. So I don't care even if I really say it. She's always mean to me and she gives me dirty looks and then giggles about it to Jenny Kelly, who hasn't the sense she was born with, Granny would say.*

– Granny would say you're the one being mean.

– *I'm not. She almost looks like she should be nice. Margery, I mean. I like her swingy smooth dark hair and that short straight nose, not like mine that bumps up . . . but you just can't tell what someone's like by the way they look.*

– Granny says that too.

– *Oh, be quiet. She's mean, that's all. One day my big sister will come – no, my big brother, even better – and tell her what's what and she'll have to listen then . . .*

Lilac's imaginary big brother and sister were called Isobel and Oliver, or sometimes James and Rachel, but never anything like Daisy or Heath. Sometimes there was just one or the other and sometimes both. They were strong and beautiful and universally popular, and they always knew the right thing to say. They had shiny brown hair that stayed where it was put, but their eyes were dark blue like Lilac's, because they were related, after all. They listened intently to Lilac's opinions, and they knew all about her fights with Margery and her frequent differences of opinion with Sister Joseph. They always, of course, agreed that Lilac was in the right.

Lilac never had an imaginary *younger* brother or sister. Sometimes she toyed with the notion of conjuring up a twin to do things with, but mostly she was happy alone with Guzzler. They had reached the brow of the hill now, and were looking down into the next bay as Lilac let the dog off the lead to range free and snuffle for traces of rabbit. The small girl hunkered down into the lee of a rocky outcrop and felt into a particular crevice in the cold, sparkling granite for a particular item. Triumphant, she pulled out the lollipop she had stashed there last Saturday, unwrapped it, and began to suck.

The taste of pink spread satisfyingly through Lilac's whole body, and her cheeks began to pucker on the inside from the sugar overload. Margery Dillon and the other girls in school could have been at the bottom of the sea, for all she cared. It was funny how, when you were in one place, it was hard to imagine that the other even existed. But then when you were called up in front of Sister Joseph and her bristly grey eyebrows, it felt as if that was your whole life, for ever, standing there feeling like a tiny worm that wanted to burrow down into the ground and never surface again.

Once the lollipop had shrunk to the tiniest possible blob on top of its white plastic stick – the hard kind with a hole through the middle, not the soft kind that you could chew and still get a taste of the flavour out of, even when everything visible had gone – Lilac did away with it in one satisfyingly violent crunch that left most of the pink in the dents of two back teeth. Probing the spiky sweetness with her tongue, she put the stick carefully back in her pocket and emerged from the shadow of the rock into the wind and the sunshine that appeared briefly between clouds. She and Guzzler started to wend their way onward along the path, only vaguely noticing some dots of people coming up from the opposite direction who would soon pass them.

The dots came closer – three adults; nobody short, no bouncing animal with them straining at a lead or running ahead. One was wearing a skirt, which struck Lilac as unusual in this weather, in this place. But she kept pace with the others and was much the same shape except for her legs, torso bundled in a navy anorak to keep out the wind, warm hat on head, shoes for walking in, not at all the sort Lilac's mother wore with skirts. It was almost as if . . . no, but that was impossible . . .

The three people were talking among themselves, carrying on a conversation about whatever it was grown-ups talked about – politics probably, or people who were sick, or something that had been on the news last night – but looking up the hill and out at the stormy sea at the same time. Lilac was suddenly self-conscious: there was nobody else on the path, so she knew they must be looking at her. She decided to talk to Guzzler, and called him, but he had found an interesting clump of mud and didn't want to come. She looked out at the sea, concentrating on a tiny speck of lighthouse almost at the horizon, as she plodded on, trying hard to ignore the advancing figures.

'Lilac McCarthy, is it yourself? And is that your big dog over there? He's a lovely one. What's his name?'

'His name's Guzzler. Because when we got him Daddy couldn't believe how much he ate.'

Lilac was so startled by this friendliness and such a normal question that she had answered without even thinking about it. Then she did think about it, and felt her cheeks start to go hot and red, the warmth prickling up from her armpits. 'But then we were stuck with him and we have to keep him until he runs under a car, Daddy says . . . Sister.' She trailed off to a mumble as reality caught up with her words.

What on earth was Sister Joseph doing out of the convent? With normal people, who were not nuns? One of them was even – Lilac glanced up to confirm her suspicions as Sister Joseph and her friends started making much of Guzzler, who had finally come over to see what was going on – a man! And not a priest or Eugene the school handyman, who were surely the only men that nuns were allowed to talk to. Except, she supposed, for maybe the doctor, if the lady doctor wasn't available and a nun had an extremely sore throat that needed antibiotics, as had happened to Lilac last winter.

A vision of Sister Joseph sitting up in bed in fuzzy pink pyjamas floated into Lilac's mind and wouldn't go away, even though she was sure, when she thought more about it, nuns must wear long plain white nightdresses like in *Little House on the Prairie*. She was still stuck trying to figure out what sort of slippers would go with that when Sister Joseph bade her a cheerful goodbye and she and her companions moved on up to the crest of the hill and away down the inland path.

Lilac felt all funny. She buried her face in Guzzler's neck

and inhaled some good deep steadying breaths of dog. Guzzler sat still and knew when he was needed. Nuns were not supposed to come out of the school and cheerily ambush you on the headland as if they were your mother's friend or a neighbour or someone. Lilac's heart was beating in her throat the way it always did at school when she might have to say something in front of the class. Then the moment would pass, and she wouldn't have spoken up, but the thumping pulse and the pre-emptive blush would take long minutes to fade away.

She straightened up and ran with the dog down, down, down the way she'd come, along the seafront, past the old aquarium, and up the hill to home, her breath scraping the bottom of her windpipe and her legs like jelly when she got there.

CHAPTER 2

The next day was Monday, and as Lilac couldn't think of a plausible illness she had to go to school. Sometimes her mother was a soft touch, if the new book was going well or her publishers were taking her out to lunch, and she would look favourably on reports of a sore throat or a bad headache or a pain in the tummy and let Lilac have a sofa day. But when her mother was at a hard bit, or a chapter that wasn't coming together, or she had just discovered that she had to go back and change everything that had happened since page 148, she wanted Lilac to be at school learning how to pass exams and get points so she could go to college and become an orthodontist. Or a radiographer. Something with a steady demand and a decent income, seeing as how none of them were going to win the sweepstakes and retire on the proceeds.

'Better send her to the Tec. to learn a trade, then,' said Lilac's father. 'Plumbers never want for work.'

'People will always need their teeth straightened,' countered her mother. 'And she won't be called out after hours for a crooked canine, either. A nice, straightforward nine-to-five, that's what she wants.'

Lilac quite liked the idea of seeing inside everyone's bathrooms, to find out what sort of shampoo they used and whether it really was normal to have a stack of *National Geographic*s beside the loo (as her father claimed), or in fact much more hygenic to keep the room as empty as possible (her mother's stance). More interesting than looking inside people's mouths all day and seeing last night's broccoli stuck in their braces, anyway. Lilac's cousin Linda said that's what *her* orthodontist found last time he tightened her train tracks.

But mostly Lilac thought she'd like to be an archaeologist, or maybe someone who designed wallpaper. She liked making new wallpapers for the rooms in her dolls' house, and then writing plays for its people to act out that went along with the designs. She was working on a teardrops-and-dragons pattern just now that would be the background for a Chinese tragedy involving a family of orphans and a mystical jade lantern.

At school, Lilac worried that Sister Joseph would make some sort of knowing comment or come up with an in-joke to signify to the rest of the class that she and Lilac were pals who spent time together outside school. Sister Joseph would think it was great, and Lilac would wish for the ground to open up and swallow her and spit her out somewhere near Tasmania, or possibly Outer Mongolia. She did her best to avoid the teacher's eye all morning and did nothing to call attention to herself. But Sister Joseph was apparently feeling charitable today and treated Lilac with her usual mixture of indifference and sarcasm. For some reason, though, it didn't sting the way it used to. Maybe it had something to do with the fuzzy pink pyjamas.

'Now, girls. You'll be paired up for the history project. I'll be assigning the partners, so you don't all need to fight over who gets Brenda McBride again.'

Brenda, the brain of the class, smirked.

'Lilac, you can work with Margery.'

Lilac stifled a gasp. Had she been wrong about the charitable feeling? Was Sister Joseph punishing her for something? Had Lilac been rude on the hill? Had Guzzler stepped on the nun's foot or drooled doggy drool on her navy nun-glove?

'Now, everyone go and sit with your partner so you can plan your research. You'll need to do some local detective work to find out more about how the town grew – and more than just asking your granny, Aisling Bond. Yes, Brenda?'

'If *I* ask Aisling's granny, does that count?'

'Yes, Brenda, that would be considered research.'

More smirking.

Twenty-eight girls stood up and tried to move seats at once, resulting in chaos as they all met in the middle. After a few minutes' hiatus and a lot of screeching of chair feet on floor tile, most of them were seated again and a low hum of conversation began. Lilac, who had not moved, looked at Margery, who had silently turned her chair all the way around so she was now facing the other side of Lilac's desk. Lilac had never been close enough to Margery before to see that her eyes were green with a tiny bit of blue right in the middle. Margery spoke first, businesslike.

'I was wondering if we could do something about the old

aquarium. You know, on the seafront?'

'You mean that blue place that always looks closed?'

'Maybe it is closed. I've never seen anyone go in. We could try to find out about its history, maybe . . .' Margery trailed off, discouraged.

'I suppose we could go by on the way home from school tomorrow and see.' Lilac was doubtful. Then she something else occurred to her. 'Or, you know Mr Mills who owns the gift shop? He does those local history walks for tourists.'

Margery liked that idea. 'He lives next door to my cousins, actually. I've seen him over the fence from them.'

'So you practically know him. Probably the aquarium's not even open. Let's do Mr Mills.'

'I can think of some questions tonight.'

'And we can go to the shop and talk to him tomorrow, maybe.'

'My dad has lots of coloured paper we could use for the display poster.'

This was OK, Lilac found herself thinking. Not fun, exactly, but OK. Margery might be quite sensible, really. If Lilac had been stuck with Jenny Kelly it would have been a lot worse because all *she* could do was giggle, *and* her handwriting was atrocious so Lilac would have been left doing all the writing for the poster. Margery was known to be artistic, so that would be a help.

CHAPTER 3

For the rest of the week, Lilac and Margery were thrown together a lot, what with one thing and another. They talked to Mr Mills in the gift shop and planned out their project satisfactorily. They somehow ended up playing tennis doubles together at PE too, and after the first few minutes close to the net Lilac forgot to worry that Margery would aim the ball right for her head with every serve. Together they advanced to the second round of the tournament on Thursday before being decisively knocked out by Lizzy Curtis and Eleanor O'Hara from fifth class. Not terribly upset, they agreed to drown their sorrows nonetheless with a Mr Freeze after school.

Sitting on the low wall opposite the newsagent's, Lilac watched Margery wrestle with the tough plastic around her stick of sweet, electric-blue ice. Lilac was already sucking on her own violet one, and feeling the corners of her mouth start to hurt from the sharp edges of the wrapper.

'Is my tongue purple?' she asked, sticking it out.

'Nearly.'

'Is it gross and disgusting?'

Margery didn't answer. Her thick brown fringe hid her eyes as she sucked all the colour out of the top three inches of her ice.

'You said *I* was disgusting.'

'What? I didn't . . . I never . . . When?' Lilac couldn't honestly swear that she hadn't, a week ago or more, but she was pretty sure she'd never said it out loud.

'At the start of school. Before you'd even talked to me. On the first day when I was new.'

This was safer ground for Lilac. 'I *never* did. Really. I double-dog swear.'

'What's a double-dog swear?'

'I don't know. But I love dogs, so double-dog must mean I mean it twice as much.'

'I heard you tell your mother at the gate that day. You said, "Margery's disgusting! I hate Margery!" and you made a pukey face. Then you started talking about your lunch, as if I wasn't even a person.'

Lilac sent her mind back to the first day of term, before the new girl Margery Dillon and her dirty looks had made any impression on her at all.

'Oh. Ohhhhh. I think I know.'

'You did, didn't you?'

'My mum gave me ham-and-cheese sandwiches, and because the butter was hard in the fridge she used Flora. I hate Flora. I told her margarine was disgusting and that I'd thrown my sandwich away.'

'Oh.'

'I got into big trouble for that. No custard on my pudding for a week because it's terrible to waste food when there are starving children in Africa.'

'In my house the starving children are in India.'

'Well they can't be in both places. They're having us on.'

A minute passed. Margery looked up. 'Have you any money left? Could we get some fizzy cola bottles?'

*****

Several Sundays later, Lilac was headed up the hill with Guzzler again. It was still mild, but the wind blew ahead of it a fine mist of rain – the sort that you'd say wasn't wet at all until you got home and found yourself soaked to the skin. Lilac was experienced with such weather, and had worn her turquoise mac over cosy tracksuit bottoms and her old runners that could get muddy. The mac made her a bit sweaty inside, but it was better being wet (and warm) from the inside out than wet (and cold) from the outside in. Her hair, in spite of a hasty ponytail, was all puffed up and had droplets clinging to its fuzziness, like a spider's web in the dew.

Guzzler looked the same as always, though he had a smart new purple lead. He had chewed through his old one when it accidentally fell off its hook one afternoon. Accusations were rife about how this could have happened, but Lilac was certain that it had been safely looped up high the last time she saw it.

At the top of the hill, Lilac stopped and looked out at the grey, cold sea for a minute. She was feeling vaguely nervous, but nothing she wanted to put a finger on. She wondered if she needed to use the loo, but that wasn't it. The horizon had disappeared in far-off mist, so that the sea and the sky merged into one another and the lone ship heading for Dublin port looked as though it was hovering in mid-air. Taking a gulp of wet wind, she hunkered down on the wet granite, stretching a hand into the crevice in the rock to see what she might find: a sign of friendship offered and accepted – or a cold, hard snub.

Feeling suddenly warmer, Lilac pulled out two Fruit Salad chews and a note saying 'Boo!', with Margery's signature love-heart-for-a-dot under the exclamation mark. She looked up to see Margery coming from the opposite direction.

'You're so late! I've been around twice already and my boots are letting in the wet. You'd better give me back one of those Fruit Salads.'

'Sorry. Daddy made me wash all his brushes at the last minute because he thinks I need to learn a trade and he's going to apprentice me as his assistant.' She handed over the booty, put the note in her pocket, and unwrapped the other sweet for herself.

'Does that mean you get to leave school?'

'No. Not even after my Inter Cert. I have to do Mummy's plan of going to college too, to have a backup.'

'I don't think my mum and dad have a plan for me. Just to not get into as much trouble as my big sister does. They just found out that Caroline's had a tongue piercing since last summer when she was going out with that boy from Gonzaga, and they're not happy.'

'Ew. Didn't it hurt?'

'*Majorly*, she says.'

'I don't think my parents would care, but I don't want to do that.'

'But maybe you will when you're fifteen. It's an awful

age, Mum says.'

They had started back down the hill because of Margery's wet feet.

'Do you want to come to my house?' Lilac asked. 'My mum bought new Nutella.'

'OK.'

Lilac had to get something off her chest.

'I met Sister Joseph up here one day. It was so weird. She was with two people who weren't nuns, and one of them was a man.'

'Did she talk to you?'

'Yes. She was normal, not like a nun at all. I was totally freaked out.'

'My mum has a friend who's a nun,' Margery said. 'A friend she went to school with. She comes to our house for tea sometimes. It's sort of strange seeing a nun in my kitchen.'

'Wow.'

'She brings us shortbread biscuits, but she says the nuns really like Coconut Creams the best.'

'What about Mikado?' Mikado were the nicest, with their squishy marshmallow and the line of red jammy stuff you could run your finger along; everyone knew that.

'I don't know. I'll ask her next time. Or you can come and ask her yourself.'

Lilac bumped Margery over a bit on the path. 'Ha ha. No thanks. You can have your weird tea with nuns by yourself, thank you.'

Margery bumped her back. 'Race you to the bottom of the hill.'

They ran.

CHAPTER 4

September

Lilac hunkered down on the pebbles and squinched her eyes at the sea, which was throwing off a million tiny sparkles, like diamonds scattered over the water. For once, the sun was shining and the sky was undiluted blue. She picked up a stone – grey, flattish, round in the palm of her hand – and skimmed it into the wavelets, but it didn't bounce. Her father's always bounced, but Lilac needed more practice.

The wind was cold but the sun was warm. The sparkles on the wave tips made Lilac think of Miss Grey, her new teacher. She was young and pretty and had a diamond ring because she was engaged, which was about the most romantic thing anyone in Lilac's class could imagine. They only had Sister Joseph for choir now, which was just twice a week, and the rest of the days the girls basked in the sunshine of Miss Grey's gentle voice, asking them sweetly to put away their pencils or take out their copybooks or to please quiet down now and pay attention.

There was a lot more talking without Sister Joseph and her ruler that used to tap errant knuckles or bop a chatterbox on the head, and Lilac wasn't sure that she'd learned anything new yet, but so far Miss Grey made a relaxing change. She was even going to take them on a class tour though it was only the start of the year, not the end, when tours usually happened. She hadn't said where they were going yet, but most people suspected it would be either the zoo or the natural history museum.

After a few more stones, Lilac decided to call it a day. She clicked her tongue for Guzzler, who had found a dead thing that Lilac really didn't want to be shown, and turned back up towards the promenade. Margery had gone to Canada for a year, and Lilac missed her. It was really unnecessary, both girls thought, because Margery could have stayed at Lilac's house. But for some reason it was more important to Margery's parents for the whole family to stay together when her father's job moved to Canada than for Margery to be near her friends and get to experience Miss Grey's class, so off they had gone in August. Lilac wondered how her mother could say, 'It's just for a year,' as if a year wasn't the most impossibly long time imaginable. By the time a year was up they'd both be eleven, which was almost twelve, which was practically a teenager.

'Mum says we can be pen-pals,' Margery had said mopily when she first told Lilac, back in May.

'But you can live in my house. We have a spare room, and we never have visitors because my mum doesn't like them.'

'I know, I told them that. But they said we all have to go. I think they want to get Caroline away from her bad influences.'

'Can't they just send her to boarding school?'

'They tried that but she said she'd run away. She can't run away from Canada. She'd get lost.'

'Do they even speak English there?'

A pause. Lilac decided not to pursue that avenue.

'Where is Canada, anyway?'

'I think it's in America. Except it's hot in America and it's snowy in Canada, so I don't know, really. I don't care.'

Lilac and Margery had determined not to believe in Canada, but as August came closer it was clear that the Dillons really would be moving away. All Margery's winter clothes were put into boxes, she was asked to pick out a few favourite books and toys to be sent ahead, and, most cruel of all, her kitten was going to live with their cousins.

'Mum said Izzy would have to spend six months in quarantine before she got there and another six months to come home again, so there's no point trying to take her. But Leo and Cormac are horrible. And what if she forgets me?' Margery was almost crying, because the kitten who had adopted her family a few months earlier had become her own personal project.

Lilac was indignant.

'If someone tried to send Guzzler to my cousins' house they'd be in big trouble. Besides, they have asthma and they're allergic to him. At least, that's what they say whenever we invite them over. Mum thinks they're just looking for excuses, but I'm not meant to know that. She says asthma is just the official line.'

Margery was distracted for a moment by the idea of cousins who didn't want to come and play.

'You mean they never come to your house? But don't they live in Dublin?'

'Yeah, over the mountains somewhere. We go to them for Christmas but they don't come down here. I think they think it's dangerous. Dad said something once about us being "beyond the pale", but I don't really know what he meant, because Shane has freckles just like me.' Lilac considered for a moment. 'Maybe if you're too pale you explode if you go outside Dublin,' she continued charitably. 'It might be sunnier down here by the sea. Maybe I'm just used to it because I live here all the time.'

'You do go sort of red in the summer.'

'I know. Shut up.' Lilac squirmed. She didn't like her pink-and-white skin and wanted to be sophisticatedly olive-complexioned like a girl she had read about in a book. Since the only olives she'd seen were green ones with little red slivers in them floating in some sort of liquid in a jar at the back of the kitchen cupboard, she wasn't entirely sure how that would look, but it sounded so much nicer than 'freckly'. Most things did, when you had freckles.

Margery was glad she had skin that turned just a little bit golden in the gentle Irish sunshine, but she didn't want to make Lilac feel worse, so she went back to the point at hand.

'So will we write letters?'

'And post them all the way? Will the postman take them? Do they have postmen in Canada? How do they bring the letters through the snow? Maybe they have sledges and husky dogs . . . will you ski to school every day, or skate down the river?' Lilac was off on a new imagining.

'I suppose I can tell you in a letter.'

So Margery and her big sister Caroline and her mum and dad had gone off to Canada at the start of August, and poor little Izzy had gone to the cousins, who were really extremely excited about getting a kitten on loan and promised to love her but show her photos of Margery every night; and Lilac had sat down and started a letter as soon as the clock moved past the minute when the plane to London (the first flight of three to get all the way there) was supposed to have taken off.

Dear Margery,

[Lilac wrote]

Hoping this finds you as it leaves me, which is what you say in a letter but I don't really know why. Maybe they mean I hope it finds you quickly. But not too quickly because you've only just gone and I don't want the postman in Canada to be confuzed and not bring it to your house because you're not living there yet. Does the postman already know you're going to be living there? Maybe if I write really s l o w l y you'll be there before I put this in the letterbox. Mum says I have to come and have dinner now but it's only leftovers so I'm not hungry. Dad says my dinner will be in the dog if I don't come right away so I'll be back in a minute dot dot dot

Dot dot dot I'm baaack. Do you like the way I wrote dot dot dot there instead of putting the actual dots? I think it's quite amuseing but Sister Joseph didn't like it when I did it in my essay about Saint Patrick last year. Maybe our new teacher will have a better sence of humour. I mean, my new teacher. I can't beleive you're going to miss a whole teacher. I hope she's a nice one, but I hope you have a nice one in Canada too.

Lilac stopped writing because her hand was getting sore, and because she was thinking about Margery's new school. There would be boys in it, Margery's dad had said. Most of the schools there had boys and girls and no nuns, unless you paid loads of money and went to private school, which could be Catholic. Which was funny because in Ireland there was nothing special about Catholic school – it was just the only school there was, and she was pretty sure it was free, once your parents bought your uniform and your books and your pencil case and things. And there were no boys after first class, and nuns were two a penny.

The idea of boys in your class was partly yucky and partly scary. Margery said she wasn't worried, but Lilac thought she was just putting it on. Boys, everyone agreed, were horrible. They burped and farted on purpose and did disgusting things like picking their nose and eating it, and sometimes they had fights in the playground and really hurt each other. There was one time Theresa Quirke had pulled Anne O'Mahony's hair so hard that she had a headache for the rest of the afternoon, and another day that Maura Rooney pushed Theresa into a puddle so her uniform was all wet and she had to sit on the radiator till home-time; but boys gave each other black eyes and broken arms. At least, that's what she'd heard.

Lilac's cousin Shane was too little to count as an actual boy, being three years younger than her, and she'd met Margery's cousins Leo and Cormac, and they seemed, well, sort of normal, but those weren't good examples of boys as a whole: boys as they would be if you had a class half-full of them. And then there were the three boys at the end of the road, the Jenningses, who went to the Christian Brothers' school. Sometimes she'd see one of them – David, probably, but it might have been Michael – wave at her through the window when she'd pass by with Guzzler, and she'd wave back. When they were five and six and seven they used to play together, football in each other's back gardens or frisbee on the grassy patch at the end of the road, but not any more, now that they'd all grown out of that sort of thing.

She went on with the letter.

I went to the supermarket with Mum this afternoon and she started singing along and dancing to the old-people pop music they were playing. I was soooo embarassed I closed my eyes, and then I walked into the apples and about 200 of them fell on the floor and they all bounced around for ages and I had to put them back up and Mum was really annoyed with me when it was all her fault. She bought some of them and she says if my apples at lunch have bruises I'll just have to eat them anyway. I'm going to have to smuggle them outside for Guzzler.

I've already crossed today off our calendar, but tomorrow I'll be good and wait until bedtime. Don't forget to do yours.

Secret sign of affection,
Lilac

She ended with a big swirly signature that she'd been practising for a while. It was a good opportunity to use it for real, because mostly she just doodled it on the inside covers of her copybooks and pieces of paper that her father left lying around the house with sketches for paintings. Then he'd come back looking for them and find *LilacLilacLilacLILAC* all over the details and she'd be in trouble again.

Lilac and Margery had bought two identical tiny calendars for 50p each in the pound shop, with a picture of a kitten above flimsy pages with a square for each day. The picture didn't change with the month, you just ripped off a page underneath it; but that was OK because the kitten was cute.

They were each going to cross off the days until the year was up and Margery came home. They also had a secret sign that was a cross between a handshake and a blown kiss, which they would do whenever they thought of each other; unless they were in awkward company in which case a shortened version was allowed, which would just be a subtle wiggle of two fingers.

CHAPTER 5

Now it was September and the new school year had started, and there Lilac sat every day in lovely Miss Grey's class; except that she didn't have anyone to talk to in the playground at break-time, or to walk part of the way home with until they got to the railway line and went their separate ways, or to meet up the hill on Sunday afternoons. It was like the old times last year, before she and Margery were friends. Except that back then, Lilac and Guzzler were content to be two, a girl and her dog; and now, someone was missing.

Lilac was meant to be doing her homework, but instead of discussing what Red Hugh O'Donnell had done – whatever it was, she rarely listened to history, which had nothing to do with her – she was writing to Margery.

Dear Margery-poos,

How are you? I am well. Guzzler ate too many apples and threw up on the rug in front of the fireplace. Daddy says he'll have to go, but I know he's only joking because I saw him petting Guzzler when he thought nobody could see.

Miss Grey is beautiful in a wispy sort of way. She has pale brown hair that she always wears up, and tiny gold earrings that I think are heart-shaped. I keep trying to imagine what her first name might be. She looks like a Cecilia. Or a Gwendoline, maybe. Isn't Gwendolyn Grey a totally romantic name? She's not very good at keeping us quiet, though. I think we're her first ever class of her own.

She's taking us on a class tour to the Aquarium to look at habitats. It's not much of a tour when the aquarium is right there on the seafront so we're not even going in a coach, but still. I didn't think it was even still open, but it is. As well as to look at habitats it's because Miss Grey says she wants to get to know us better. I think she won't like us so much when she's had to run after Theresa Quirke on a school tour. Remember the year she got lost at the zoo? Still, Miss Grey is nice so far. And not ANYTHING like Sister Joseph. What's your teacher like?

Secret sign,

Lilac

She folded the page over itself into thirds as evenly as she possibly could and went to find an envelope and a stamp. You needed special stamps for Canada, so it couldn't just be the sort that went on a birthday card to your cousin in Cork. She rummaged in the drawer of the bureau by the front door until she found the right one, scattering rubber bands and twisty ties and those mysterious pieces of green string with metal things on the ends as she went.

They had a half day off school for teacher training, so even after she'd given Red Hugh some of her attention there was still time to go for a walk before it got dark. 'I'm just taking Guzzler out,' Lilac shouted to the house in general as she let a happy dog bound out the front door. Her mother called something vague in return but wasn't really paying attention. She had just received the latest paint-colours catalogue and was busy circling all the names she liked best. Then she would go through them again and see if any of those were attached to nice colours, and finally she'd walk through the house reimagining the rooms in her chosen hues. She never bought any paint, because Lilac's father painted only on canvases and never on walls, but she liked to think about it when she was stuck on a plot for her book.

Lilac had several things planned for today's walk. First, she was going to look in the window of Panache Boutique, which would have some new cardigans on display. In spite of its fancy name, the boutique only ever appeared to sell cardigans and boring skirts and tweedy trousers. Every week Lilac liked to look at the new stock and pair each cardigan with an appropriate teacher at school. After that, she was going to explore a new route to the seafront. Miss Grey might get lost on the way to the Aquarium, not being really from around here, and then she – Lilac – could come up with a short cut and get them all there in record time.

She needed to be prepared.

Lilac turned left to go up to the main street, walked past the newsagent's and the pound shop and the shoe shop, and then paused, pulling back an impatient Guzzler, at Panache. The fluffy lavender one for Miss Grey, she decided, and the red bumpy one for the teacher across the hallway. The black-and-white checked one for the secretary in the school office, and the long blue one with the pockets for the junior infants' teacher who was always losing her chalk. Nuns didn't wear cardigans, so none for Sister Joseph. Lilac's mother said all the clothes in Panache were at least two seasons out of style, but she had also often said that none of the teachers at Lilac's school had an ounce of fashion sense. Lilac could almost always pinpoint at least one teacher for each cardigan, so evidently her mother was right.

That task done, Lilac turned down one of the lanes, the one between the florist's and the supermarket, because it probably led straight to the seafront but she'd never gone down it before. Guzzler was used to taking a different route on every walk, and there were new cat smells down here, so he came happily enough. At first there were big, elegant, old houses, but then they turned into smaller, newer ones with the glass in the front windows cut up into little diamond shapes, and glass porches around the front doors with just enough space in them for a doormat and a potted plant on a stand.

Finally the narrow road became so narrow that it dwindled to a pedestrian passage with a black metal pole in the middle to make sure nobody would think of driving down it. Even without the pole, only a Mini would fit through, or one of those tiny Fiats like Granny's old car – and it might get wedged and never be able to reverse, and then everyone walking their dogs or riding their bikes would have to clamber over the stuck car until it rusted away to nothing.

Grey walls rose on either side of the passage, and if Lilac hadn't been with Guzzler she might have had the impression that it was a bit of a lonely spot where she didn't want to dilly-dally. There was a funny smell, and empty chip bags and a drink can left by the wall. But it opened out quickly to the main road, and as Lilac had hoped, she came out right on the seafront by the Aquarium.

The old building looked quite run-down, which was why Lilac was always surprised to hear it was still open for business. Lilac remembered going there a few times when she was little, but not for years now. It was mostly painted blue, to be like the sea – but not like the real sea that was there right beside it, which was much more often silver and grey and no describable colour at all. The bottom part of the walls were covered with fat, white-painted pebbledash that was falling off in big clumps so you could see the flat grey plaster underneath.

Lilac perused the posters outside, thinking they made it look more like a cinema than a place with real live fish and animals on display. The pictures showed blobs of jellyfish, and big grey fish with spots, and even some penguins.

Jellyfish washed up on the beach every summer; Lilac used to scoop them up with her bucket and spade and throw them back into the water, never touching them just in case they were the stinging sort. Big grey fish were not interesting, because they were neither brightly coloured nor dangerous like sharks. But penguins . . . penguins might be good. She would like to see the penguins. She imagined a miniature landscape of ice and snow, with penguins waddling like clowns, slipping and tripping and running into each other until they got to the water, where there would be tiny icebergs floating around for them to swim to and pull themselves up on, only to slip and trip and fall off again. Yes, she was looking forward to seeing the penguins.

The door of the Aquarium opened and a man in a black suit came out. As he came down the ramp towards her, Lilac realised it was Father Byrne, the curate. He was assigned to the boys' school, so Lilac didn't see him often outside the holy confines of the church, but she knew him well enough to recognise. ('Lovely Father Byrne,' her mother always said. 'He sort of *glows*, up there on the pulpit. It must be God's grace shining down on him.')

She knew that you shouldn't dislike a priest, but she had always thought Father Byrne was a little slimy. He was much younger than any normal priest, for one thing, being probably in his mid-thirties, with a full head of slicked-back black hair and a sort of orangey complexion. He ran the folk-music Mass on Saturday evenings – the newfangled 'vigil' Mass that the old people didn't think counted as real Mass at all – and he played the guitar. That just didn't seem right to Lilac: in her world, priests should always be grey-haired and a little vague, and prefer the violin, if anything.

Father Byrne patted Guzzler as he passed, and said 'There's a great fellow' to him, and nodded in a distracted way at Lilac. She gazed studiously at the penguin poster, hoping very hard that he wouldn't decide to stop and have a conversation with her. She needn't have worried: he hurried on his way and crossed the road to go back up to town. She wondered why the priest would be at the Aquarium at all, unless maybe the boys' school was going on a tour there too.

CHAPTER 6

In Miss Grey's classroom, Lilac was sitting opposite Agatha, the new girl. Brenda McBride had left because the McBrides had moved house, and Margery was gone of course, and Agatha Kovac had joined the class. Agatha's family came from Hungary, which had prompted some bad jokes on her first day about whether they had enough to eat. Agatha had turned pink and it was clear she was trying not to cry. Miss Grey hurriedly showed everyone where Hungary was on the big map of Europe on the wall – and then when it turned out to be beside Turkey there were some more *hilarious remarks*, as Lilac told Margery in a letter afterwards, as if Agatha couldn't understand what people were saying about her. In fact, she spoke perfectly normal English, as her family had lived in Ireland since she was six months old, and they had just moved up from Carlow at the end of the summer.

Agatha had wavy dark brown hair that always looked messy, as if she had just taken off a woolly hat and couldn't find her hairbrush, and she reminded Lilac somehow of a bird, with delicate bones and a slightly sharp nose. Lilac thought she was *interesting*, and wanted to know more about her, but she didn't want to do anything obvious like asking Agatha to play elastics at lunchtime in the playground. Not straight away, but in a little while when her soft country accent had worn off a bit and the mean girls had moved on to a new target.

But now Miss Grey had put Lilac and Agatha at the same table, and Lilac regularly let Agatha borrow her purple pencil sharpener as an indication that her feelings were friendly. She put it meaningfully on the junction of the two desks to show that Agatha was welcome to take it without asking any time she liked. This made it fall through to the floor at least three times a day, and then one of them had to scramble underneath to get it, which was always a nice distraction; though if Sister Joseph had been teaching she'd soon have put a stop to that sort of thing.

Miss Grey, however, was not noticing a quiet girl disappear under her desk now and then. She was too busy gently asking Theresa Quirke to stop talking and to pay attention to her map of the world because she had put the Arctic and the Antarctic at the wrong ends, and there were no tigers in Africa.

Miss Grey moved back up to the top of the classroom and tapped a piece of chalk on the board for silence. Silence was slow in coming, and just as everyone finally began to pay attention, Agatha bumped her head on the desk trying to surface too quickly after one more purple-sharpener retrieval mission, which led to another flurry of giggles all round.

'Agatha! Young ladies do not sit on the floor. I'll have to

give you a black mark.'

Miss Grey was clearly at the end of her tether, to do such a thing to the quiet new girl. Agatha looked alarmed and Lilac tried to shoot her look of sympathy and solidarity. Shooting a look was something she'd read about more often than she had actually ever done, and from where Miss Grey was standing, it looked as if Lilac had rolled her eyes.

'Lilac, I saw that,' she said reprovingly.

The rest of the class was agog, watching the two goody-goodies get their comeuppance, and Lilac was mortified. She glued her eyeballs to the textbook as her cheeks got warmer and warmer. She knew exactly the shade of deep pink flush that was growing there, and was sure everyone was staring at her; which of course made the embarrassment last longer than ever. Finally, her cheeks stopped burning and she unclenched her toes inside her shoes.

Miss Grey had started to say something about a concert, but she was cut off by the bell that rang to announce lunchtime. The noise level rose instantly as everyone continued the conversations they'd been having all along but were no longer bothering to whisper, so she just shook her head gently and left the room, saying ". . . after lunch, girls."

Lilac and Agatha's tentative friendship had progressed to playing elastics in the yard at lunchtime. The other end of their rope of rubber bands was tied around a tree trunk, as they didn't have a third girl to provide another pair of legs. They could have asked someone, but they didn't want to be turned down.

'England, Ireland, Scotland, Wales,

Inside, outside, donkey's tails'

they chanted, as first one and then the other jumped in and out and over and onto the stretched elastic bands. Agatha paused at donkey's tails.

'What's your favourite animal?'

'Dogs, of course. I like penguins too. Do birds count? But I'd still have to say dogs first, or Guzzler would be hurt.'

'Guzzler?'

'My dog. He's highly intelligent.'

'Oh. What sort of dog is he?

'A big one. He has a bit of Great Dane in him, and a lot of sheepdog and some other bits of something else. Maybe poodle, for the woofliness. We don't know what his parents were, exactly.'

They switched places for Lilac's turn jumping, this time with the elastics up at Agatha's knees, and the other side higher on the tree trunk. The tree was slightly uphill from where Agatha was standing, which made it more challenging. Lilac did England, Ireland, Scotland, Wales, and paused to take a breath before tackling the next set of jumps. They were pretty sure the elastics would snap on donkey's tails, when you have to stand on them, so she was just putting off the evil hour when they'd have no game.

Lilac said, 'What's yours?'

'My what?'

'Favourite animal.'

'The pangolin.'

'Isn't that a musical instrument?'

'No, it's like an armadillo, sort of. They're really cute.'

'Can you have one for a pet?'

'No, they're just in zoos and encyclopaedias. I've never seen one in real life.'

Lilac thought it was sad to have a favourite animal you'd never even met. She hadn't seen penguins often, but they were only her second-favourite, after all. And she was going to see some on the Aquarium trip.

'Maybe you should pick a cat or a guinea pig or something instead, then. Then you could have one. Animals are good. I mean, it's good to have a pet. They listen to you when nobody else does.' She suspected she was doing a bad job of explaining just how important a member of the family Guzzler was. 'It's like . . . well, he's basically my favorite person, even though he's not a person.'

Agatha looked as if she was about to say something, but then the bell rang and they had to go in. The elastics were still in one piece because they'd never finished the game, so they'd be able to play again tomorrow. Lilac had used up all her mum's secret box of rubber bands to make that set, and they had already snapped and been tied back together so many times that one more break would make them too short to use, and then she and Agatha would have to come up with a new game.

When school was over, Agatha lingered by Lilac's coat hook, fiddling with the zip of her schoolbag while Lilac gathered her various belongings and stuffed things into pockets. Lilac wasn't sure what was happening, but Agatha appeared to be making a friendly advance of some sort.

'Are you walking home today?' Lilac asked.

Agatha looked relieved.

'Yes. Are you as well? Do you want to walk with me? We go the same way, a bit, I think.' Lilac knew that was true, because Agatha usually passed her in her mum's car on some part of her route. She hadn't been certain that Agatha had noticed, though.

'Sure. My bike has a puncture so I have to walk.' They went down the school stairs in harmony, shoes clattering on the pale-green Formica tiles, and out the double doors at the front. Small children scattered ahead of them, because the junior infants' classroom was below theirs. Agatha and Lilac smiled down at the little ones, so cute in their tiny school uniforms, and felt very grown up.

'Lilac, can I ask you something?' Agatha began.

'Um. OK.' Lilac wondered where this could possibly be going. Questions that needed a pre-question were almost always unpleasant.

'Do you like Rancheros?'

'Yes. Actually, I love Rancheros.'

'That's what I thought,' said Agatha happily.

Lilac found this mysterious. Mum certainly never put Rancheros into her lunchbox, and they hadn't been making bar charts for maths about what sort of crisps people liked best.

'How did you know?'

'I just knew. You have an aura.'

'Oh, right.' A moment later, she asked, 'What's an aura?'

'It's a sort of colour I can see around you. Yours tells me that you like Rancheros and Hubba Bubba.'

Lilac wasn't too fond of bubblegum, but she let it pass.

'I can't see any colour around you. Do only some people have auras?'

'No, everyone has one, but only some people can see them. My mum knows about it. She taught me.'

This was fascinating. 'I thought your mum was a violin player,' Lilac said. Agatha had mentioned that her mother sometimes played in concerts, which sounded exciting to Lilac; but then Agatha thought that having a father who painted pictures was somehow special, when it was perfectly ordinary as far as Lilac was concerned.

'She's lots of things. She's definitely sort of . . .' – Agatha searched for the right word – 'flowy.'

A picture popped into Lilac's mind: a woman standing dramatically on the top of a cliff, long copper-coloured hair blowing out behind her, wearing a medieval dress with sleeves that opened up at the ends and were so long they touched the ground. Such a woman would have the wisdom of Solomon and the knowledge of the ancient peoples and the beauty of . . . of . . . who was it again? Pandora? Lilac wasn't sure, but Pandora sounded pretty.

'Wow.' Lilac's own mother suddenly seemed drab by comparison, even though she was normally quite passably interesting.

They walked on in silence kicking at dry leaves now and then, and at Lilac's turning Lilac said 'Bye' at the same moment that Agatha said 'See you.' And then they went their separate ways; but it was a comfortable sort of parting, not a rushing-away-in-relief sort of one, and Lilac hoped Agatha would loiter by her coat hook again tomorrow.

CHAPTER 7

Margery's letters to Lilac had not been entirely satisfying. There had been one good one just after Margery's family had arrived in Toronto, and then a postcard with a picture of distant snow-capped mountains with autumn-coloured leaves in the foreground, and the caption 'Fall foliage in Ontario'. Lilac had to look up 'foliage' and was used to seeing 'fall' as a verb, so this took some decoding to begin with. The other side was written in their secret code but Margery had forgotten to send the key, so until she did there was nothing Lilac could do about reading it. She was pretty sure it would just say something like 'Aren't these mountains pretty?!?' anyway, judging by the punctuation at the end.

Lilac still faithfully looked at her cat calendar every night, and wrote letters, but more as if they were diary entries than letters that would get a reply. Still, it was nice just to write things down sometimes, and putting on stamps and pushing a letter into the postbox felt important. She did get a paper cut on her tongue once from licking the envelope too quickly, but she learned a valuable lesson and always gently dabbed at the gluey edge after that.

The idea that it would be all right to be friends with Agatha – sort-of-best friends, even – was beginning to be something Lilac could think out loud to herself without feeling terribly guilty. But she wasn't quite sure what to say to Margery about Agatha. Agatha knew about Margery, of course, because her name came up in school every now and then, and someone would say explainingly, to Miss Grey or whoever had asked, 'She was Lilac's best friend.' And then everyone would look sadly at Lilac for a moment, as if she had lost a leg or something. Lilac was getting a bit tired of that, really.

So, somehow, Lilac had never mentioned Agatha in any of her letters. Not by name. She might have said 'we' once in a while, or 'one of the other girls in the class', or 'the new girl who's sort of from Hungary', but she wasn't quite sure at this point how she could tell Margery all about Agatha's interesting mother and what auras were, because that sounded too familiar, somehow. So she hadn't said it yet, and she always thought she'd just leave things as they were for another week.

On Sunday afternoon after Lilac had finished her weekend homework, she decided she had to write to Margery and work the subject of Agatha in there somehow. She was tired of feeling like a double agent. She couldn't work for both sides at once. This was war, and she had to choose. She knuckled down to the task, imagining the smart navy uniform she would wear with its gold trim and all the medals that would be pinned to her lapel.

No, wait, this wasn't war. What was she thinking? Anyway, as a spy she would have to be undercover; though she could wear her uniform for the award ceremonies so they could pin on the medals, she supposed. Or maybe her true role wouldn't be revealed for decades, until she was an old woman and her grandchildren would ask, 'Nana, was that really you who did all those dangerous things?' and she'd nod her snowy white head sagely and tell them that it was, and they'd be just like Lilac was now, trying hard to imagine it all.

Dear Margery,

[she wrote, while she was thinking, just to get started]

If we were in a war would you rather be a spy or a doctor? Or a general telling the armies where to attack?

[She wrote the next bit extra fast to get it over with, holding her breath.]

Agatha (who is the new girl and who I have been playing with a bit sometimes lately now and then in between times when it's break time and I've no book to read) thinks she would be one of the people who runs like the wind from one army to the next to tell them the news of how the battle went, but I don't think they have those any more. She says sometimes the electricity goes out in a war and running is the only way to send the glad tidings. (Or the tragic ones.) What do you think? Does Canada have wars? Since Ireland is neutral I would have to be a spy for one of the other countries — maybe I could come over

41

there and help out. They'd never suspect a ten year old, and it would be good training.

Love from Lilac

And then she breathed out hard and found she was a little dizzy, and she ran and got an envelope and a stamp straight away and stuffed the page in, along with a cute pony notelet she had swapped with Katie Byrne for a tiny rubber that smelled of strawberries but she had two of. And she stuck on the stamp and licked the back (carefully) and thumped it down with her fist and put it on the hall table where the next person who was going out would find it and take it with them to post.

It was chilly on Thursday morning. Miss Grey's class walked briskly from the school to the seafront in a long snake of navy uniforms under variously coloured coats. They waited outside the Aquarium while Miss Grey talked to the employee behind the ticket office window, and then they streamed in to the muggy building, shedding anoraks, unfurling scarves, and tying jumpers around their waists.

'Did you see Maura and Theresa trying to bunk off?' Lilac nudged Agatha as they and some of the others ranged themselves around a large tank full of pebbles and water, vaguely wondering what might live there.

'They weren't bunking off, they were just dawdling, I heard them tell Miss Grey.'

'Of course that's what they told her. But they were trying to get left behind so they could go to the shops instead.'

'Oh. But then the shop people would see their uniforms and know they were meant to be at school, wouldn't they?'

'Yes, but they wouldn't do anything about it.'

'Really?' Agatha had assumed that Neighbourhood Watch extended to catching schoolgirls on the mitch, but apparently not. 'But you'd know that they knew, and you'd feel really guilty.'

'I would, but I don't think Theresa and Maura ever feel guilty.' Lilac looked around, wondering what they were supposed to be doing. 'Is there even anything in this tank?'

'I don't know. We're waiting for the person to tell us, I think.'

'I want to see the penguins. Let's go and find the penguins.' Lilac scanned the room for any indication of where the penguins might be, and started to break away from the gaggle.

'Lilac, Agatha!' said Miss Grey, returning to the group instead of trying to round up everyone at once, 'Stay right here. Miss O'Sullivan is going to tell us about our native fish species. Come over here, everyone!'

Lilac made a face at Agatha. The penguins would have to wait.

Dear Margery,

We went to the Aquarium. The fish were boring, but never mind about them. I really wanted to see the penguins. And when we finally found them they were waddling about looking totally cute and pompus at the same time, but the poor little things were on bare earth instead of snow and ice like they should have been. They had water to swim in, but it obviously wasn't properly cold.

There were no iceburgs at all, not so much as an ice cube floating in it.

Even if Mum calls the weather Arctic sometimes when it's freezing in January and the pipes burst and all Dad's canvases get wet and ruined (which only happened once, actually), the Irish climate is obviously not right for penguins. And these penguins are expected to live in our Aquarium all year round, not just in December and January. I'm afraid they'll die because they're in the wrong habitat. We just learned all about the Antarctic so I know where they're meant to live.

I tried to ask the lady that works there about it but she wouldn't listen to me because she was watching Maura Rooney slide down the handrail at the stairs, and then Maura fell off and dropped her can of Fanta and it spilled all over the floor and then all our shoes were sticky because we had to walk over it to get out again. And then Miss Grey said it was time to leave and we got back to school early and she still gave us homework which wasn't fair because everyone knows you don't get homework when you go on a school tour.

Do you have an aquarium in Canada? Or is it so frozen that there's no water for the fish to swim in?

Love, Lilac

CHAPTER 8

Dear Margery,

The weather's horible.

Is your postman sick? Maybe you haven't got any of my letters. Maybe your mother is hiding them from you because she thinks we're plotting to overthrow the goverment. Maybe the Canadian police are spying on you and they think I'm a dangerous influense so they're taking away all my letters.

Do you have a new friend?

Lilac

Lilac went downstairs and buried her face in Guzzler's curly rough back fur. He was the only one who understood what it was like when your best friend moved away and didn't even seem to bother writing back to you. At least, she felt like he understood, even if that had probably never happened to him.

*****

'Now, girls, I have something exciting to tell you,' began Miss Grey. This opening always heralded something new in the line of schoolwork, although not everyone agreed with Miss Grey about what qualified as 'fun' or 'interesting'.

'We're going to do a careers project!'

Smiles and eye-rolling commenced, equally distributed around the room. 'Aisling Bond, what do you want to be when you grow up?'

Aisling looked unhappy to have been picked on first. 'Um,' she said. 'Errr . . .' Lilac thought to herself that in Miss Grey's shoes she would not have chosen Aisling for her first victim. Aisling was more a follower than a leader; she liked someone to plant the idea first so that she could join in. Lilac put up her hand, and wiggled it a bit in case Miss Grey missed it.

'Wait a moment, please, Lilac. Agatha, how about you?'

Agatha was indecisive. 'Maybe a ballerina . . .'

'Lovely!' Miss Grey said brightly. '. . . But, well . . .' Sister Joseph would have caustically reminded Agatha that she was no longer in senior infants, and that she needed to be more practical. Miss Grey, though, was wary of destroying children's dreams, and was fond of telling them all that they could be anything they wanted if they just worked hard enough. Her examples were usually along the lines of scientists and vets; she did seem to be trying to steer them away from the princess and Wonder Woman ideas that had been perfectly acceptable just a few years earlier.

'I want to be a model!' shouted Adele Duffy from the back row. Adele was tall, with long brown hair that she tossed from one side of her head to the other every 45 seconds or so, and her mother liked to enter her into competitions. She claimed that she had been a Billie Barry Kid when she was three, but since they moved out of the city her parents couldn't bring her to rehearsals any more so she had stopped. Nobody was quite sure whether to believe her or not, but they'd all seen the Billie Barry Kids at the pantomime in the Gaiety every Christmas and they could imagine Adele fitting right in.

'Please raise your hand, Adele,' said Miss Grey. 'A model! I see.'

Lilac fluttered her hand even more enthusiastically.

'Lilac,' said Miss Grey finally, with resignation.

'I want to be an archaeologist. And an interior decorator. And I'd like to be an actress. And I want to invent things so I think I'll be a scientist too.'

'That all sounds very . . . busy, Lilac. Maybe you should pick just the one to start with. Now,' she continued, to the class at large, 'you're all going to make a poster with pictures and descriptions of your chosen career, or one you think seems interesting. If you can't choose, I can make some suggestions. I'd like them to be realistic, so please don't choose princess because that's quite unlikely, and it's not a career, as such.'

Lilac was feeling contrary.

'Miss Grey, why is being a princess not a career? If you worked really hard at finding a prince who wanted to marry you, couldn't you become a princess? And isn't it good to work hard for your dreams?'

Miss Grey's shoulders slumped a little but she remained upbeat. 'Let's try to think of careers that you can go to university to study for.'

'When I grow up I think I'll be a university professor who teaches people how to find princes who want someone to marry,' Lilac said.

Miss Grey took a new tack. 'Let's think about jobs our parents and other grown-ups we know have. For instance, I can think of a grown-up in the room right now who has a career some of you might be interested in.'

'A teacher,' chorused a fair number of the class, happy to finally have an obvious answer.

'Maybe some of your fathers – or mothers – would like to come in and talk to us about their jobs and how they studied hard at college or trained for a long time to get them.'

'My mam works in the newsagent's,' announced Laura Devine. 'She saw an ad in the window and they said she could come in and have a go, and the next day they gave her the job even though she got her sleeve stuck in the cash register and it jammed the spring, and they had to unscrew the whole drawer to open it up again and *then* all the coins fell out on the manager's foot and broke his little toe.'

'Well, yes,' said Miss Grey. 'Your mother is welcome to come and talk to us. I'm sure she meets many interesting people in her job. Anyone else?' She looked pointedly at the people whose fathers had what she thought of as proper jobs. Lilac was never sure where her parents fell on this scale, but she wasn't looked at, so she decided that artists and writers weren't proper enough jobs for Miss Grey today. Her parents might be on the backup list of people to ask once the ones who worked in offices turned out not to be able to come in because they had to be at work.

*****

When Lilac was on her own going home, she had a choice of routes. If she went through the town on her way home from school, she passed by the church and all the shops. If she went around by the coast road, where the Aquarium was, it was a little further, but sometimes she liked to see the sea, stretching out greyly to the horizon, flat and far and unbroken. She could put her annoyed feelings at Miss Grey for that day's injustices, or her hurt feelings at Margery for the lack of letters, or her grumpy feelings at her dad for being grumpy, into a little imaginary boat and push it down over the crunching stones onto the water and then run back up without wetting her feet and watch it all float away.

Other days she didn't need to do that, and then she walked more quickly through the town, pushing her bike and enjoying the warm, coloured lights and bustle in the dank wintry weather.

CHAPTER 9

There was going to be a Christmas concert to raise money for the Aquarium. It turned out the real reason Lilac's class had gone there was that the Aquarium wanted all the schoolchildren to see how old and sad it all was, so that they would want to help raise money. It should be a big joint effort, because the Aquarium was for the whole community, they said, and if tourists came to see it that would be good for all the shops and restaurants and the whole town.

All the schools were to be in the concert – Lilac's school and the boys' school and the girls' secondary school as well. Miss Grey's class were having special extra choir practices with Sister Joseph, and they had to stay back after school on Wednesdays to get things exactly right.

'Why is the concert in the church if it's not a Mass, Sister Joseph?' asked Theresa Quirke pertinently (and impertinently too). 'Why don't they have it at the Aquarium, in that big space where they don't have the dolphins any more?'

'Because that's the building that needs a new roof, Theresa,' Sister Joseph replied acidly. 'If we're charging admission, we need at least to guarantee that the audience won't be rained on while they watch us. Also, you are not dolphins.' Agatha tittered at this, and then blushed to be the only one who appreciated Sister Joseph's wit.

'But then, why can't we sing Duran Duran, Sister? If it's not a holy concert?'

'Because it's in the church, child.' Sister Joseph looked down decisively and rustled through her sheet music to indicate that the conversation was over.

Theresa Quirke looked downcast. Lilac tried and failed to imagine the whole class singing 'No-No-Notorious' while Sister Joseph conducted. Sometimes she suspected Theresa asked questions even when she knew the answer would have to be no, just so that she could say the name of her favourite group out loud.

Sister Joseph was what Lilac's father would call a stickler. This meant things were never exactly right, as far as she was concerned, which made Wednesday after school a painful experience all round.

'Pay attention, young ladies. I'm not just drying my nail varnish up here, you know.' This was a joke, since of course nuns had short nails without so much as clear polish; but Sister Joseph delivered it in such a sarcastic tone of voice that there were no smiles at all. Everyone just muttered under their breath about how they couldn't watch her mark time and look at the the music too.

Sister Joseph gave up trying to conduct, started the metronome, and sat down at the piano. Usually Miss Taylor, the junior infants' teacher, accompanied them, but she was out sick today. 'And one and two and three . . .'

Lilac enjoyed belting out the songs, and so long as the girls on either side of her were reasonably in tune, so was she. They were supposed to learn the words off by heart, so that they could watch Sister Joseph swishing her hand up and down in time to the beat and all stay together, but so far most of them hadn't managed that. Without a conductor, the practice wasn't much of a success and after a little while more Sister Joseph frustratedly let them go home a bit earlier than usual.

Lilac and Agatha walked home together, as they usually did now. Lilac pushed her bike, and they balanced Agatha's bag of books on top of Lilac's on the back carrier. Every time the bike bumped up or down a kerb the bag would fall off, but they'd put it back again because it was still nicer than carrying it. After a few times Agatha started holding the bag in place, but that made talking awkward because then she was walking right behind Lilac. She moved around to the other side of the bike so they were diagonal from each other instead.

'What I think,' Lilac announced as they walked, 'is that the concert money should buy a new habitat for the penguins. Urgently. I'm surprised they've survived this long in such bad conditions. They need snow and ice and icebergs and –' she waved one hand around, making the bike swerve so that Agatha had to clutch the bag to stop it falling off '– and Antarctic stuff.'

'Poor flightless birds,' Agatha agreed. 'They can't fly to somewhere colder. Not even through the holes in the roof that we have to raise the money to fix. Could we help them somehow? I mean, before the concert, soon? We could bring them some ice, maybe.'

'Or ice cream, for snow. They could eat it and slide on it at the same time.'

'I'm serious. They're suffering. What else is cold?'

'I'm serious too. Well, maybe not the ice cream. But how can we bring ice to the Aquarium without it melting? Do you have one of those big cooler box things people use for camping?'

'No. We don't do camping. Do you?'

'No, we don't either. My mum, and camping . . .?' Lilac shuddered melodramatically at the idea. 'Yours, though. I thought your mum was all close to nature and stuff. Wouldn't she love camping?'

'Why did you think that? No, really not.'

'But the auras, and . . .' Lilac realised that the vision of the lone woman communing with the winds on the clifftop was all the work of her imagination. Agatha had never actually described her mum that way.

'When I was little,' Agatha said, 'I used to think she was magic, maybe a witch, because she'd talk in this weird language that I sort of understood but it didn't sound like real words. But eventually I realised she was just swearing in Hungarian.'

'So you speak Hungarian?' Lilac was impressed.

'I understand it pretty well, but I don't really speak it. Though I can probably say the bad words. If I wanted to.'

'Oh. That's a pity. I thought for a minute we could maybe have it as a secret code. I like secret codes.'

'But then you'd have to learn it too.'

'Oh. Yeah.' Lilac pushed on, avoiding crumbling bits of pavement where the rain had got in and clumps of bright green moss were starting to grow. 'My dad swears at his paintings, and at Guzzler, and especially when Guzzler gets into his studio and knocks over his paintings and steps on his tubes of oil paint. But I'm not meant to know what he's saying either. I don't think my mum knows any swear words.'

'I think they all do, they just pretend not to,' Agatha said, considering it seriously.

'Even nuns?'

'No. Not nuns.'

'No. Sister Joseph probably says "Fudge" when things go really badly wrong. And then she has to tell the Mother Superior and she gets into trouble.'

The idea of Sister Joseph stubbing her toe and yelling *Fudge!* was too much. They giggled all the way past the shops to Lilac's turning, where they said a quick goodbye because the gentle drizzle was making them wetter than they had expected.

It wasn't exactly getting dark yet – the street lights weren't on – but the day was definitely gloomy, and the lights in the houses Lilac passed looked yellowly warm and glowy. She put one foot on a pedal, hitched herself up to lean against the saddle without throwing the other leg over, and freewheeled gently along the path the rest of the way home, keeping a wary eye out for dog poo and thinking about ice cream.

CHAPTER 10

Miss Grey sent home forms for parents to fill out if they would like to come in and talk about their careers, to help with the projects.

'So she's throwing the field wide open, is she?' said Lilac's father gruffly. 'Well, it's not my sort of thing. Maybe your mother will do it.'

But Lilac's mother said she had a meeting with her publishers that day. Lilac thought it was probably a hair appointment, but she didn't really mind. It was a bit uncomfortable, the thought of her mother at the top of the classroom as if she was the teacher, telling everyone how they could be a writer if they worked hard enough and wanted to with all their hearts and . . . but all Lilac could really imagine her mother telling them was that they should all go to college and get a nice reliable nine-to-five job, maybe as a legal secretary or an optician, depending on their exam prospects.

'Would you like to come to my house for tea on Sunday?'

Lilac had been practising asking, nonchalantly, as if it was a perfectly ordinary question. It *was* a perfectly ordinary question. She didn't know why it was so difficult to ask, except that she had the idea that Agatha was going to say no, and then it would all just be awkward. She could tell by how long it was taking Agatha to answer that she had been right. Here it was, awkward already. Lilac babbled on, trying to paper over the squirmy feeling, trying to give Agatha an easy way out.

'You probably have stuff to do on Sunday, don't you? Or you could come some other day? Or we could meet up the hill, except that the weather's too horrible these days . . .' She turned her windfall apple over and over, looking for an unbruised part to bite into.

Agatha was taking a breath in, trying to say something. Their words clashed and neither of them heard what the other had said. Lilac stopped talking. Agatha tried again.

'I'm scared of dogs.'

'You're scared of dogs?'

'Mm-hm.' She said it so quietly that Lilac had to strain to hear what was coming next. 'A dog nearly bit me when I was little. I don't really remember it but my mum says that's why. When a dog comes near me, or I think one's going to, I sort of panic.'

Lilac hadn't thought of this, in all her imaginings about what might make Agatha not want to come over. Guzzler was so much part of Lilac, part of home and life, that she found it hard to imagine a house without a Guzzler, never mind a person being scared of him.

'But Guzzler's lovely. He'd never hurt anyone,' she said.

'I know. It's not about Guzzler. It's just dogs.'

Inspiration struck Lilac. 'We can put him outside. If I put him in the back garden while you're there, he won't be around. He can go into the shed if he's cold. I'll put his bed in there and show him so he'll know what to do. And I can explain it to him so we don't hurt his feelings. He's highly intelligent.'

Even though this was exactly the opposite of what her father always said, it was what Lilac always told people when describing Guzzler. Her father didn't know Guzzler like Lilac did. Guzzler understood every word, and lots of things that weren't even said. And anyway, it hurt his feelings when people called him stupid.

'I can't,' Agatha whispered, concentrating intently on peeling every tiny bit of pith off the segments of her mandarin orange. 'I'd know he was there. I'd be afraid he'd get in.'

It seemed she was not for turning. Lilac didn't know what to say next. If it had been Margery, she was pretty sure that the next thing would have been Margery inviting Lilac to her house instead, but that didn't seem to be happening.

The bell rang and they went back into the classroom, both of them heaving private sighs of relief that the conversation had been ended, and tossing the remains of their fruit into the bin on the way through the door.

*****

Finally, there was a real letter from Margery, the envelope so thoroughly stuck closed that Lilac had to go to the kitchen for a pair of scissors to cut it open.

Dear Lilac,

I am really really really sorry I haven't written back yet. Canada is really cold. School is strange and Caroline is acting wierd. It's so hard to explain that I didn't want to write until I knew more about what I was trying to say. But I really like getting your letters and I'm glad you have a friend called Agatha because I have a friend too. His name is Paul. He's a boy but it's okay to have a friend who is a boy here because boys are just normal people in your class. I have to do my homework now but I will write again soon.

Love from Margery

Lilac stomped around the house a bit after she'd read the letter. She wasn't sure what she thought about it. Things being strange didn't seem like a good enough reason not to have written back for so long, and Caroline always acted weird, and Lilac didn't see how boys could possibly just be normal friends. She took Guzzler for a walk, but today gazing at the sea didn't provide her with any answers, and she was still in a grump when they got home.

The next day there was another letter. Lilac was surprised, and a little worried because she hadn't answered the first one yet.

Dear Lilac,

I felt bad about not writing but then when I had written I felt much better. So now I'm going to write more. I should probably wait until I have a letter back from you but I'm not going to. Like when Caroline says she doesn't have the patience to wait for a boy to ring her so she just rings him instead. She says that sometimes it works and sometimes it turns out it was a bad idea. But you're not a boy and we're already friends, so I think it'll be OK.

Caroline's school here doesn't have any boys and mine does. Caroline's school costs lots of money and has a uniform but mine is free and I can wear whatever I want except my skirts have to be down to my knees. Her school is not like Degrassi Junior High, and mine sort of is. Exept that mine is a Nelmentery school not a junior high, and hers is a high school and a private school. I think Mum and Dad sent Caroline to that school so she wouldn't meet any boys, but all the girls at her school are crazy about boys and now Mum thinks that she should have gone to the regular public school instead and Mum and Dad had a big row about how they're spending all this extra money on private school when I wasn't meant to be listening cos they thought I was outside on my roller skates but I'd come in cos I grazed my knee and I was looking for a plaster when I heard them.

I got roller skates because Caroline got a walkman. Mum and Dad are being extra nice to her. I went to a roller disco birthday party. It was fun but I didn't know most of the music and everyone else was much better at skating than me. They said it's because of hocky but I don't understand how hocky would make roller skating easier. Caroline played hocky last year at home but she can't skate either.

Love from Margery

Lilac considered stomping some more, but she was interested in school in Canada and wanted to know more. She had been running out of things to say to Margery in her one-sided correspondence, but now she was full of questions.

Dear Margery,

Is it snowy? What do you wear to school? Does everyone look at you to see if you've got the wrong sort of jeans? What is Caroline's uniform like? Are there men teachers? Are there no nuns at all or only a few? What colour are your roller skates? Everyone here wants a Care Bear for Christmas but I don't think I'm going to get one because I never do until I get something a bit like it but worse two years later. Anyway, I think they're a bit babyish. Miss Grey says I'm quite mature for my age. But I think she says that to people when she wants to make sure they keep being good in class because she can't keep control over the ones who are bad. She said it to Agatha too (which is probably true) but then I heard her say it to Jenny Kelly yesterday and that's definitely not true.

[She decided not to ask about Paul so she didn't say anything else about Agatha.]

I got new socks with hearts on them and a duffle coat. We have a careers project and parents are coming in to talk about their jobs, but not my parents because they don't have real jobs, Miss Grey probably thinks.

I'm happy you wrote back.

Lilac

CHAPTER 11

Lilac arrived late on the morning that the parents were coming in to talk. She had been at the dentist's. She was annoyed with the dentist for saying she'd have to come back for a filling, and annoyed with her mum for sending her for a checkup this particular morning, because she'd rather have missed a regular morning, with maths and Irish, than the careers talk morning at school.

Rachel Jackson's dad worked with computers, and he would be talking first. Miss Gray said this was exciting, but Lilac couldn't think of anything that sounded more boring so she didn't mind not being there. But then Agatha's mum was going to talk about being an actuary, which was apparently what she did when she wasn't being a musician.

Lilac didn't know what an actuary was, exactly, but she assumed it was something 'flowy', like sticking pins in people to make them feel better, or making the little dolls to stick pins into if you want someone to feel worse. Though come to think of it, she wasn't sure that second part was a job people really had. Or the first part either, really. She was looking forward to seeing the Aura Lady, as she thought of Agatha's mum, though, and finding out about the needles.

Lilac went into the classroom trying to be quiet and quick at the same time, but she tripped over the sweeping brush in the corner by the door and heard the clatter as it hit the nature table on the way down, scattering pine cones and autumnal leaves all over the floor. She felt her face go red and picked everything up without looking at anyone, letting her messy curls swing over her eyes so that she couldn't see them even if she'd tried. She finally got to her place, pushed her bulging schoolbag under the chair and put her bottom on the seat. Only then did she dare to look up. Rachel's dad was still talking. Lilac couldn't see why she might need to know anything about computers. Hardly any jobs needed anything to do with computers, and Lilac certainly wasn't planning to have one of those, in real life or for her project.

'Thank you, Mr Jackson', said Miss Grey. Some of the girls clapped politely while others took the opportunity to continue whatever conversation they'd been having between parents' talks all morning. 'Next, Mrs O'Herlihy will be talking to us about her job as a solicitor. Who knows what a solicitor does?'

Lilac was pretty sure a solicitor sent people letters that made them cluck their tongues at the breakfast table, but she didn't want to say that. She looked at the parents ranged at the back of the room, but couldn't see Agatha's mum with her long hair and swirly dress anywhere. Maybe she would arrive a little later.

Mrs O'Herlihy was a large lady who took her time arranging herself on the small chair placed at the top of the classroom. Lilac was afraid she'd topple over on one side or the other, but she didn't seem to be wobbling once she'd got comfortable. She had pink lipstick and fluffy brown hair and a friendly face, and she didn't look like someone who would write worrying letters.

It turned out that solicitors help people buy their houses, and they sign documents, and sometimes they go to court to help people not have to pay their parking fines. Talking to the judge in court sounded exciting but the rest of it did not, no matter how much Mrs O'Herlihy tried to make it seem like something they might all want to do. She said if you liked reading and public speaking it might be a good career to consider, and Lilac did like reading, but on the whole she would rather find something else more fun to do her project on, never mind spend her life at. She was pretty sure she was going to do her project on either palaeontologists or vets.

Agatha's mum didn't come after all. Agatha said, afterwards, that there had been an emergency at work but she didn't know exactly what. Lilac imagined a patient lying on a hospital bed with giant needles sticking out of his back.

'Miss Grey,' Lilac asked after the parents had gone home. 'Are there any penguin experts in Ireland? The lady at the Aquarium didn't really seem to know much about penguins. What about at the zoo? Are the penguin keepers there like her or actually experts on penguins? Would that be a penguinologist? I think I'd like to be a penguinologist ...'

Miss Grey tried to tackle Lilac's first question, but she didn't know the answer. 'You know, Lilac, I'm not sure. Let me see if I can look it up and let you know.'

Lilac was not much impressed. How would Miss Grey look it up? Lilac was well able to look up 'penguin expert' in the Golden Pages – in fact, she had done that last weekend, and there were no entries.

'Do you have a friend who's a librarian who will tell you things librarians won't tell other people? Because I asked at the library and the lady at the desk sent me to the encyclopaedias, but there was nothing about Ireland under Penguins.'

'Well, no, I don't. But I do have quite a good encyclopaedia at home.'

Lilac knew that Miss Grey would come back the next day saying she couldn't find anything out and that maybe Lilac should do her project on some other job instead, like Librarian or Journalist. She started to think maybe she'd do Opera Singer, because her parents were going to the opera at the weekend, so there were definitely opera singers in Ireland. Maybe she could find one to talk to.

CHAPTER 12

'Lilac,' her mother had said in a no-nonsense tone that morning, 'Dad and I are going to the opera next Saturday. Jeannie McGrath is going to come to babysit you.'

'Who?'

'You know, Jeannie McGrath. Eileen-McGrath-from-the-tennis-club's daughter. She's about sixteen, I suppose. She goes to the big school.'

'Oh.'

There wasn't really anything else to say. Before Lilac's granny had moved to Cork, if her parents went out they'd drop her over to Granny's house. She took her pillow and her sleeping bag and stayed up while Granny watched the first half of the *Late Late Show*, and then Granny would kiss her goodnight and shuffle her weary bones (she said) out of the room, and Lilac would snuggle down on the sofa in the glow of the red lampshade with the little bobbly fringe. The bobbles reminded her of the dark-pink fuchsia flowers in Granny's garden, with their fat bells hanging down.

When she was much smaller, her parents would pick her up on their way home, at midnight or even past it, her father slinging her over his shoulder, sleeping bag and all, into the back seat of the car, and up the stairs to her own bed. She'd pretend to be asleep the whole time, but she wasn't. Each step of the stairs went bump bump bump with the hump of his shoulder under her tummy, and in the car she'd flutter her eyelids to see the orange and white streetlamps turning into streaks of light as they went by.

When Lilac got too big to be carried like a sack of potatoes, they generally left her at Granny's all night and picked her up the next morning. But then Granny moved to Cork and a succession of babysitters, usually teenage daughters of her mother's friends, came to chivvy her to bed too early and refuse any requests for chocolate biscuits.

On Saturday night Lilac was busy sorting her large collection of Bunty comics into piles according to story artist. This was not a useful way to keep them, but since she had started noticing some distinctive artists' styles in the stories, she wanted to do something with that information. She ignored the doorbell when it rang.

'Lilac! . . . Lilac! Answer the door! That'll be whatshername.'

'But I'm upstairs.'

There was a hesitant knock, in case the bell didn't work.

'I'm changing, Lilac, please get the door.'

'O . . . K . . .' she stood up on her bed, careful not to disturb the many papery piles ranged around her, and thumped downstairs in her socked feet.

The heavy door pulled back slowly to reveal a teenager

mostly hidden under thick brown hair and glasses.

'I'm Jeannie,' the teenager said.

'I'm Lilac.' Lilac stood back to let Jeannie come in. Jeannie took off her navy-blue anorak and hung its hood over the knob at the end of the bannisters. Lilac liked her style. Not her clothes – they were uninteresting – or her hair, which was too frizzy; but the way she looked like she knew what she was doing and didn't care if it was wrong.

'We don't put our coats there,' Lilac said apologetically. She took the anorak and hung it on the coat hooks in the hall press.

'Jeannie, there you are,' said Lilac's mother, coming downstairs in a silky blue dress, jewellery gently clinking and a delicious smell wafting in her wake. 'Now, Lilac's bedtime is nine o'clock. Help yourself to a cup of tea and a biscuit, and watch television if you like, of course. We should be home by midnight. Lilac will show you where everything is. Mwah, darling.' This last was directed in Lilac's direction with a blown kiss so as not to disturb freshly applied lipstick, as she put on a floaty mauve scarf and then her long warm coat. 'Gerry! Are you ready?'

Lilac's father appeared from somewhere at the back of the house, looking oddly buttoned up in a tweed jacket and a knitted tie. He nodded at Jeannie and said, 'Be good, Lilac, night night.' And they were gone.

Lilac and Jeannie looked at each other, assessing. Jeannie had a book in her hand, but it was a novel, not a schoolbook. Lilac decided to put on her good manners, at least for now.

'The kitchen's through here,' she said, leading the way. 'There's the kettle and the teabags, and the biscuits are in the tin with the kittens on it and the hidden chocolate is in the press at the top there. The milk is in the fridge. The spoons are in this drawer here.'

'That's all right, I won't have anything till later, thanks,' said Jeannie.

Lilac liked this. She was showing Jeannie around her model home. She went through the door to the sitting room.

'This is where the TV is. I usually sit in this corner of the sofa.' She gestured towards the permanent dent from her bum. 'But I was sorting out some stuff upstairs when you came.'

'Well, that's OK. I'll just read my book,' said Jeannie, settling herself easily in the other corner.

On the one hand Lilac was happy that she could just go back to what she'd been doing, but on the other, her piles of sorted comics had somewhat lost their allure. She lingered, but didn't know what questions counted as rude. What she really wanted to know was if Jeannie had a boyfriend, but she couldn't start there.

'Where do you go to school?'

'In the town.'

'The one with the navy uniform or the wine one?'

'Navy.'

'I've seen those coming up the hill when I come home late after extra choir rehearsals. Are you going to be in the concert for the Aquarium too?'

'I s'pose so.'

'What year are you in?'

'Fifth.'

'I'm in fifth class. Did you go to my school for primary?'

'No, we moved here when I was in second year. We lived in Kilternan before.'

'Where's that?'

'Nearer to Dublin, sort of in the mountains. There's a ski slope there.'

'A ski slope? With snow?' Lilac had never heard of people skiing in Ireland.

'Artificial snow. It's the only one in the country.'

Jeannie didn't seem chatty, and Lilac didn't know anything about skiing, so she ran out of conversation. 'Well, I'll go back upstairs, then.'

'OK.' Jeannie was already flipping her book's pages to find where she'd left off.

Ten minutes later, sorting comics was definitely boring. Lilac put her favourite pyjamas out on her pillow, neatly folded and angled just so, and tidied up her room a bit. She decided she should tell Jeannie that they had two sorts of milk in the fridge, just in case she preferred one or the other in her tea. She went back down. Jeannie was staring out the window with her book on her lap, looking a million miles away. She hadn't heard Lilac's feet on the stairs. Lilac went back up the last five steps and came down again more noisily, because she didn't want to make Jeannie jump.

'Do you have a boyfriend?' It just slipped out, she hadn't meant to ask. But Jeannie looked as if she was thinking about the boy she was madly in love with.

'Nope,' said Jeannie. 'I don't think any boys live around here. There isn't a boys' secondary school in town, but there are two girls' ones.'

'There are boys who live up the road. The oldest one takes the train to his school.'

'Well, yes, I suppose there are *some* boys. There must be.' Jeannie didn't sound all that convinced. 'But I only know girls, and all my mum's friends have girls. Maybe nobody around here had a boy the year I was born.'

'Maybe.' It did seem strange, now Lilac thought about it. She mostly knew girls too. That's what happened when all your school was girls.

'My friend Margery has gone to Canada for a year and there are boys in her school. She says it's weird.'

'Yeah, it would be.'

Since Jeannie didn't seem to be particularly busy reading or making tea or whatever else babysitters were meant to do, Lilac decided she'd better entertain her.

'Do you want to see my room?'

'OK.'

Lilac showed Jeannie the piles of comics and explained how she'd been organizing them. She showed her the ornaments on her special shelf that was high up so nothing would get broken. She didn't show her the little diary with the lock where she sometimes wrote down what she'd done all day, or her toadstool piggy bank, for security, because there were seven pound notes and 52p in there.

Then she and Jeannie watched *Knight Rider* until it was time for bed. On the whole, it had been a good babysitter night.

CHAPTER 13

Dear Lilac,

Caroline nearly ran away. I think they gave her the walkman because they were afraid she'd do something like that and they were trying to make her happy. But it didn't work. She left a note saying she hates Canada and she was going to fly home and live with her boyfriend. But she took the bus, so Dad drove to the airport and he got there first and waited at the Airlingus desk until he saw her. Nobody's talking about it now — he just drove her home and she went to her room and hasn't come out since yesterday. Mum is trying to be all normal, but her voice keeps squeaking.

I think they're going to let her go to the high school that's free, where there are boys, instead of the private school. Dad said at least if she has a boyfriend here she won't run away. Mum said then we may as well not have come to Canada. Caroline is going to say that she's in love with Danny at home and still doesn't want to stay. I don't know if she's really in love. Danny has an earring and a sort of a little moustache. I didn't like him when I saw him at the shopping centre that day when she went all pink and started giggling.

Since I got used to the idea that we're here for a year, I don't really want to leave early. I don't want to have to pack everything again, and changing schools in the middle of the year is a pain. I hope Caroline decides she wants to go to the other high school.

Maybe you should get the Aquarium to send the penguins here in the winter. We're all going to learn to ski and skate and everything. There's no snow yet but Dad says it's going to be colder than I could ever begin to imagine in my wildest dreams. I'm going to try to have a wild dream about snow tonight to see if he's right.

Love, Margery, sister of The Tormented One

Lilac was quite horrified by Margery's letter. This was a highly dramatic situation. Her imaginary big sister Olivia would never do such a thing. She couldn't really imagine Jeannie the babysitter doing it either. But Margery sounded as if it was all pretty much normal, so Lilac supposed she shouldn't make too much of a big deal about it either. And to be honest, though she missed Margery, it might be awkward being friends with Agatha as well if Margery came home before the big gap of the summer holidays, which would change everything anyway, because they always did.

She was also quite confused about the logistics of whatever Caroline had been planning to do.

Dear Margery,

How was Caroline going to get a plane ticket when she got to the Airlingus desk if your dad wasn't there? Did she have money? Can you just buy a ticket right before you go? Mum always arranges our holidays in February and we don't go till August. Though that's the car ferry to France if we don't go to a farmhouse b and b in Kerry. Maybe planes are different. Don't you need a travel agent to do it?

If you came home now you'd have to do the career project which is awful because I still don't know what to write about. And you'd have to learn all the words for the songs for the concert really quickly. So it's probably a good thing to be staying, really. That's a good idea about the penguins, though. I wonder can they go on a plane? (Then they wouldn't be flightless birds, har har.) Did you know people go skiing in Dublin on artificial snow? You could have learned before you went so you won't fall over in the winter.

Love,

Lilac

CHAPTER 14

The career project was due next Monday and it was Thursday already. Maybe the Aquarium lady would do after all, even if she wasn't – evidently – an expert on penguins. She had some sort of job, obviously, which could be described for project purposes. Lilac went home by the seafront and re-examined all the posters on the wall outside the Aquarium before walking up the long ramp to the ticket booth and knocking on the glass. The woman inside it looked up at Lilac, looked back down at her *Woman's Way*, sniffed, pointedly opened the cash drawer and closed it again, and finally said, 'What?'

'I was wondering if I could talk to the lady that works here showing people round. I'm doing a school project on careers. She's a zoologist, isn't she? Or . . . an aquariumologist?' Suddenly, Lilac wasn't as sure as she thought she'd been.

'Can't go in without a ticket. Student?'

'Yes.' Duh, thought Lilac. I just said I was doing a school project. And I'm wearing a uniform. But she kept her polite face on the outside, just in case it still mattered.

'One fifty during the week. But we're about to close. I'll let you in for 50p.'

'Oh, thank you!' It was just as well she'd kept her polite face. Lilac rooted in her schoolbag for her pencil case and triumphantly found the 50p she'd got from the tooth fairy. It had bits of coloured-pencil shavings clinging to it, so she blew them off before handing it over. A pink ticket came back to her through the dip in the counter under the window.

'In you go. Ten minutes.' The woman jerked her head towards the door, and Lilac pushed her way into the gloomy, swimmy building.

On the class trip two weeks ago, the atmosphere had been noisy and chaotic, with everyone laughing and pushing and running from one exhibit to another. Miss Grey stood in the middle warbling 'Oh, don't rush off, girls,' and 'Why don't we all stay together and look at one thing at a time?' Lilac had seen the fish and the penguins and the other exhibits, but hadn't really noticed what the Aquarium itself was like.

Today, the building was almost totally silent, with a vague hum and an underwater feeling all over. The shiny pale-blue paint was peeling off the walls, and the handrails were losing their paint too, showing rusting dark metal underneath. In three places there was a bucket or a plastic tub on the floor to catch the drips from the ceiling when it rained. The lighting was too dim to let anyone see the carpet, but Lilac was pretty sure she wouldn't have wanted to examine it too closely. Theresa's Fanta was definitely not the only sticky liquid that had soaked into it in the past weeks, months, or even years, and it pulled ever so slightly at Lilac's soles as she walked. This aquarium had seen better days, that was for sure. Lilac went down the corridor past some uninteresting tanks that displayed nothing but pondweed behind foggy glass, and turned the corner to the penguin habitat.

There were the penguins once more, in sad little clusters of two and three, muttering to each other about their disgraceful conditions and how they'd make a complaint to the management if only they had opposable thumbs to hold a pen. At least, that's what it looked like they were saying. Lilac took a closer look at the explanatory sign displayed by the penguin-height wall:

The humble penguin is a flightless bird of the Artic.

Penguins eat fish.

A penguin's wings are actually flippers for

swimming in the water.

'The humble penguin' indeed – why, they were quite majestic birds. What a strange description. Whoever made the sign couldn't even spell 'Arctic'. And shouldn't it be Antarctic anyway? Unimpressed, Lilac looked around for the Aquarium lady but there was nobody to be seen, so she continued up the ramp to the next set of tanks and the seashore exhibit. It seemed silly to have a seashore exhibit when they were right by the sea and anyone who wanted to see the seashore could just leave the building, but then maybe they would miss the helpful and informative signs, Lilac thought scathingly. Or maybe they couldn't afford to put in an exhibit that was any harder to look after. This way, if the seaweed died or they ran out of periwinkles, they could just send someone out the back to get new ones.

There she was! Lilac spotted the woman who had shown her class around the Aquarium the day they came, bending over another low wall and feeding some small fish to bigger fish. Lilac was taken aback by the sight. 'How do you decide which fish get eaten and which ones get to stay alive?' she asked, suddenly imagining some sort of fishy gladiator games.

'Oh no, we don't feed them our own fish! The woman laughed heartily, and Lilac felt a bit silly. She really wished she could stop to think before she spoke, sometimes.'We buy these fish. They're just for eating, not for exhibiting. Have you lost your family, pet?' she went on, looking around to find whoever Lilac should be with.

'No, I'm just on my way home from school. I wanted to ask you about your job, because I have to do a careers project. I was here last week with Miss Grey's class,' she added, so that the lady wouldn't tell her about all the fish again. 'Do you have any brochures or magazines I could use to make a poster?'

Lilac knew how school projects worked. The best marks were not awarded for lots of complicated details, but mostly for nice colourful pictures pasted neatly onto a big poster beside a few basic sentences that were neatly written and easy to read.

'Oh, well, let me just finish up here and we'll see what we can find in my office. Are you sure you're allowed to be here all on your own? The lady evidently believed Lilac was about six, but she was certainly friendly. Her frizzy blonde hair bounced when she talked, and she was the type Lilac would think of as 'motherly', which meant nothing at all like her own mother. The badge pinned to her blouse read 'Sue O'Sullivan'.

'I go past here every day. My mum's not expecting me yet.' Lilac's mum was deeply engrossed in second drafts and back stories. She would only notice Lilac hadn't come home when Guzzler started barking for his dinner, and Lilac knew she'd easily be back before that happened.

The office was behind a dark green door marked 'PRI   E'. Lilac wondered if they could only afford one set of letters for the sign, so maybe there was another office somewhere else in the building with VAT written on it. Inside, Sue O'Sullivan rummaged in the papers scattered on her messy desk and finally pulled a rumpled publication out of the rubbish bin. 'Ah, here it is! This is what I thought you might like – *Zoology Today*. Plenty of nice pics in this one. Don't mind the coffee stains.' Some of the pages were stuck together with brown stains, but Lilac took it by one corner and tried to leaf through the magazine. It looked all right.

'Oh, and here's a good one–' the woman reached up and pulled a sheaf of papers off the top of a tall metal press '– *Underwater Times!*' It brought with it a thick layer of dust, but once Lilac had blown that off there was a beautiful blue-and-yellow scene showing divers and tropical fish. Lilac could imagine nothing further from what they'd seen at this aquarium, but it would be perfect for her poster.

'Thank you! Are you a zoologist, then? I wasn't sure.'

'I'm a marine biologist, love.'

'OK. So not a penguinologist specifically, then.'

'No, because I look after all the animals, not just the

penguins. Though of course I know what to feed them and how to tell when they're sick and that sort of thing too. With all these leaks in the roof they catch cold sometimes, poor pets.'

This was the perfect moment for Lilac to bring up her worries about the penguin habitat, or at least mention the spelling mistake in the sign. But somehow she couldn't see how to do it without being rude. Sue was being so friendly and helpful that Lilac didn't want to sound critical, and the Aquarium was so obviously in need of repair that they couldn't afford to improve any of the animals' accommodations.

They talked a little more about what you had to do to be a marine biologist and all the interesting places Sue had gone when she was training, and all the other ones that would have been warmer and more exotic but she hadn't managed to go to. This led into a long and dismal story of how badly the Aquarium needed money, and how the Aquarium had nothing but bad luck ever since something that happened years ago . . . Lilac had mostly stopped paying attention as Sue rambled on about the hard times that had been fallen on, so it was a relief when an announcement came over the speakers saying that the Aquarium was closing, and she could get away politely. Sue O'Sullivan walked her to the exit and waved her out the door, and went back to looking after the jellyfish, who were next for feeding.

Once Lilac got home, she snaffled a big sheet of paper from her dad's supply, cut the nicest pictures out of the magazines, and spent a long time crafting the words 'Marine Biologist' in giant bubble writing with little frilly borders and shadows and stripes. She'd write something over the weekend, but she was pleased to have it started. The heading was always the most important part anyway.

Lilac's mum was frying sausages for dinner. No matter how carefully she watched them, they always burned. It was something to do with the pan, she said. Lilac and her dad were used to sausages that were dark brown all over and black in places. The burny taste was part of them.

'I went back to the Aquarium today,' Lilac said as she scraped the thin skin off her boiled potato.

'Lovely sausages, Nuala. I like them crunchy on the outside.' Gerry put a big glob of bright yellow mustard on his plate and dipped a chunk of sausage into it. Lilac winced. 'Were you scoping it out, Lilac? To see what they should do with the concert money?'

'No, I needed some stuff for my careers project. I'm going to do it on marine biologists because that's what the lady there is. Though I did see all the things they need to fix too.'

'Oh, I think Kathleen Jennings – you know, up the road, with all the boys – I think her sister works there. Is that who you met?' Nuala said.

'Mum, I have no idea; I didn't ask her who her sister is. Her name was Sue something, and she gave me some magazines to cut pictures out of.'

Gerry was staring into the middle distance and snapping his fingers, a frown on his face. 'There's something . . . something that reminds me of . . . the Aquarium, and money . . .'

'Yes, they need money. We know that.'

But something else . . . what was it now . . . ? He pointed

his knife at Lilac with a flourish. 'Got it! There was a sweepstakes ticket, years ago, that was lost.'

'Sweepstakes? Like the big prizes?'

'That's it. The hospital sweepstakes. I remember hearing a story that the Aquarium staff had all chipped in on a ticket, and they claimed they'd won, but the ticket couldn't be found and so they were never able to pick up the money.'

'Oh, that must be what she was telling me about when she was talking about all their bad luck. I'd sort of stopped listening. So now we have to put on a concert to save them instead.'

'Seems like it. But you'd have to do a Christmas concert anyway. At least this is for a good cause.'

'Sure. Or we could just find their missing sweeps ticket and get to go home early on Wednesdays.'

'You do that, then. Pass over the butter for my spuds, please.'

CHAPTER 15

On Monday, Lilac handed in her project with minimal writing and maximum artfully cut-out pictures. Miss Grey looked vaguely at it, said 'That's nice, dear', and put it in the pile of projects. Lilac could see Rachel Jackson's on top, with a heading of 'Computer Programming – The Next Big Thing' in green bubble letters. It had no pictures at all, and lots of tiny writing, so obviously it would get a low mark.

There was a letter from Margery at home. Lilac opened it eagerly, looking forward to the next installment of Caroline's adventures.

Dear Lilac,

We had to make a diorama for a project. They said it was a project in a shoebox, so I made my poster and folded it up and put it in a shoebox, but that wasn't right and now I have to do it all over again. How was I supposed to know that? Even though they speak English here sometimes things are so different that it might be easier if they didn't. At least then people wouldn't expect me to understand everything.

Maybe I'll have to be a nun. You don't need good marks for that, do you?

That was a JOKE.

Did I tell you Caroline's at the school attached to mine now? The regular high school. She's happier about it, I think, though she's still not talking to us so I can't tell for sure except that she hasn't run away again for a week. I don't know what's going on with her love life. But I know she hasn't got any letters from Danny because I check the postbox every day before she comes home and there's never anything for her. I don't know if she writes letters to him, though.

Teenagers are majorly strange. What will it be like when we're teenagers? Will we be as weird as Caroline?

Love from Margery

Lilac hoped she and Margery would be more like Jeannie McGrath when they were teenagers, maybe, than like Caroline. Jeannie seemed easier to deal with, more like a normal person and less like an alien from another planet. Except that of course, in Lilac's fantasies of her own future, she was glamorous and beautiful and tall and slender and less square-shaped and mop-headed than Jeannie.

Lilac's mother said that Jeannie was going to turn into a swan some day, when she learned to stand up straight and pulled back her hair, but Lilac couldn't see it herself. She tried standing up extra straight but it didn't seem to make any difference for her, when she looked in the mirror. Maybe she always stood up straight. She probably had excellent deportment, that had to be it. She tried balancing a book on her head, but it fell off when she looked in the mirror, so she sat down to write a letter instead.

Dear Margery,

A project in a shoebox sounds like a stupid idea. I don't think Canadian marks will count when you come home, don't worry. Unless you get good marks after this and you want them to. But if you tried to do a project in a shoebox here Sister Joseph would have had something to say. Not in a good way. I don't know what Miss Grey would say because she's not as sarcastic as Sister Joseph so she'd probably just say Oh Dear Margery, That's Not Quite What We Need Is It?

I saw the penguins again and they still make me sad but there's nothing I can do. Grownups don't listen to kids saying they're wrong, they just give out to them for being rude. Maybe after the concert we can ask if they'll fix the penguin habitat instead of making a new dolphin enclosure.

Guzzler sends a snuffle. He misses you, I think. He liked when you gave him your biscuits.

We will never be as weird as Caroline. She has cornered the market, my Dad says.

Love from Lilac

CHAPTER 16

'Gerry! Where's your father, Lilac?'

'I don't know, Mum, I just got home.'

Lilac's mother's writing was going well, which meant she was in her ratty pyjama bottoms because she had only half dressed, and she wasn't too clear on what time of day it was. Lilac knew this was a good thing because even though Nuala (that was her mother's name) moaned and groaned every second time they saw her about how she wasn't getting a thing done and it would never be finished, every other time she mused happily about all the lovely family time they'd have together when the book was done.

When the book was done, of course, there'd be other things that had to happen, like shopping for something to wear for lunch with publishers, and cleaning the house like a madwoman because someone was coming to do an interview, and more writing because now someone needed the outline of the next book, or a short story, or a book review – but in general, Lilac knew, it was a positive sign.

'Gerry! . . . Did he go out?'

'Mum, I don't know. I didn't see him. If he's not in the house, then I suppose he's out. Didn't he tell you?'

'I don't know, maybe. I might not have been noticing.'

'Well, maybe he left a note. He knows you don't hear things when you're working.'

Lilac looked at the kitchen table and the countertop and scanned the random pieces of paper covering both surfaces for anything that might be a note from earlier. One possibility said 'No. 53' in her father's writing, and another held a diagram that might have been an idea for a painting or some sort of directions or map to an undisclosed location, but usually if he was going to leave a note it was less cryptic and more practical – 'Gone for teabags', that sort of thing.

Then she looked into the back garden. It was starting to get dark, but she could still see all the way to the end wall. 'Guzzler's not there. Dad must've taken him up the hill.'

'Oh, that'll be it. But I wanted to ask him something. I'd better write it down. Have you done your homework?' her mother asked her vaguely, belatedly.

'I just got in, Mum. I'll start it after I watch *Fortycoats*.'

'Make sure you do, then.'

Lilac was mostly in charge of herself these days, though someone else usually made sure there was dinner at some point in the evening. She quite liked it that way, though it did mean she'd nobody to blame but herself if she left her homework too late and had to get up at six the next morning to do it instead.

An hour later, homework mostly done, Lilac was back in the kitchen rummaging around for a stopgap bowl of cereal. There was still no sign of her dad or the dog, and her mother hadn't re-emerged from her lair of words, as Lilac amused herself by calling the office. She was going to put it in a letter to Margery, next time enough had happened to warrant a letter. She was collecting funny stories from school, but Sister Joseph had been so distracted by the preparations for the concert that she hadn't even made sarcastic comments to Adele Duffy in the past week or so. It was an odd thing about writing to Margery: Lilac always worried she didn't have 'enough things' to talk about, but then most often the letter ended up being about something else entirely, once she got started.

The front door banged and Gerry came in, windswept and wet. He hadn't much hair, so it was hard for him to look windswept, but somehow the angle of his collar and his scarf conveyed it quite well. He was frowning, which was not unusual, but he wasn't his normal laid-back self.

'Lilac! Where's the dog?'

'What? Guzzler's with you, isn't he? You took him up the hill.'

'No, I didn't. He didn't eat his lunch and when I called he wasn't in the garden. I've been shouting for him all over the town.'

A sick feeling lurched into Lilac's stomach. She looked at the Frosties in front of her and pushed them away. It was as if she should have known this was coming, but she hadn't.

'He would never run away. Never.'

'I certainly didn't think he'd go that far from his food for so long. That's why I went out to look.'

Lilac raised her voice to a wail. 'Muuuuuummmmm!

Mummmmm! Guzzler's missing! What if he's been knocked down? Or fallen off the cliffs? Or been hit by someone who was throwing stones on the beach? Or eaten raisins and got really sick and is hiding somewhere we'll never find him being totally miserable? Or . . .'

'Now, Lilac, don't work yourself into a tizzy,' said her dad, who was some way to being in a tizzy himself, except it was harder to tell with him because his natural state was practically horizontal. 'Nuala!'

The panic in their voices must have got through Lilac's mum's concentration because all in a clatter she practically fell out the door of her office and halfway down the stairs to them. 'What? What's happened? Are you hurt?' and then, as she saw them both whole in body but creased of forehead, 'What is it?'

'Guzzler seems to be missing, Nuala,' said Lilac's dad. 'He didn't eat his lunch and I've looked all over town for him.'

'And there's no tag on his collar,' Lilac remembered. Guzzler usually wore a round tag with his name and their phone number on his purple collar, but the link of chain attaching it had snapped a few days earlier and nobody had yet gone to get a new one made at the little shop on the corner where they cut keys and repaired shoe heels.

Lilac wasn't sure what she expected her mother to do – either throw up her hands in despair and wail, or scold them for breaking her flow and say that the silly animal would be back any minute. Instead, she sat down at the table with a new look in her eye, almost as if this was a challenge she knew she could rise to.

'Don't worry, Lilac, we'll find him. Now, Gerry, where

exactly did you look?'

Lilac's dad explained his route – all the places they often walked with Guzzler and the corners he particularly liked to nose around in.

'Gerry. Ring the Guards and notify them. Lilac, get the phone book.'

'Do you really think the Guards pay attention to lost dogs, Nuala?'

'Well, this is our lost dog, and he's important. Make sure you let them know that.'

'Right, so.'

'And then ring the ISPCA and tell them, and ask them who else you should contact. Where else will anyone who finds a dog go?'

'Lilac,' (Lilac had come back with the phone book) 'can you go out and ring the doorbell of every house on the road and ask if they've seen him? I know you're feeling wobbly, darling, but it will get better if you start doing something. Take the big yellow torch with you, and call his name every time you go out on the street. Ask the people if you can shout for him in their back gardens too. You know how he can get over the back fence if he really wants to.'

'OK, Mum.' Lilac took a deep breath and stepped forward on legs that weren't sure what they were for. 'What are you going to do?'

'I'm going down to the beach. Gerry, follow after me when you've made the calls. Lilac, come back here when you've finished the houses and wait in case anyone rings. Make sure you take your key in case we're still out.'

Lilac's mum belted up her long coat over her ratty pyjama bottoms, stepped into her wellies that lived in the coat cupboard, took the other torch, the green one, from the shelf, and went forth into the wet darkness of November.

Lilac's stomach was still churning, but she was glad to have a job. She found the yellow torch, miraculously where it was supposed to be, and put her coat back on. It was still damp after walking home from school in the mizzle, and the cuffs were cold and clammy on her wrists. She felt guilty to care about that, when her poor lovely sweet puppy was out in the dark, wet evening, somewhere lost and miserable, but she couldn't help making a face about it. She stomped out the door in her boots, feeling an eensy bit heroic all the same.

She called 'Guzzler! GUZZLER!' as she went from one house to the next. Some of the neighbours weren't home yet, their houses still dark and unwelcoming; some had glowing lights and shadows running to and fro behind the curtains; others had a porch light on a timer that had come on even though they were out, so that Lilac wasted precious moments on the doorstep just in case. The whole time, she shouted, in between breathlessly explaining herself and being led through homes into back gardens.

The neighbours were helpful and sympathetic, but they were deep in their nice warm, dry lives without a dog, let alone a missing one. On any other day, she'd have been delighted to see inside all these houses that were the same shape as hers but each so differently employed, but today she couldn't spend time thinking about that. Every time she stepped out into a back garden, she wanted so badly to see a fuzzy dripping shape come hurtling towards her that she kept imagining it about to happen, and was bitterly disappointed over and over again when it didn't.

By the time she'd finished all the houses, her head was thumping and her stomach was full of giant lumps, all the way down from her throat. Her eyes were burning and she had stopped trying to hold back tears. It was raining properly now anyway, so nobody could tell the difference in the dark. Her voice was getting scratchy and in between shouts she had to cough to make them work.

She came back up the hill towards home, more miserable than she ever remembered being. Truly miserable, not even giving some brain power over to thinking about how miserable she was or how she would describe it to Margery later. With her whole mind, she was willing every shadow to turn into dog, her dog, her wet, lovely, slobbery, terrible dog.

Then there *was* a shadow, but it was the size of two people and couldn't possibly have been a dog. It was her parents coming back up from the beach, still as dogless as they'd gone. Lilac didn't realise until she saw them that there had been a place inside her that was holding onto the idea that Mum or Dad would find Guzzler and he'd be back home before she even got there. The stone in her throat turned into a boulder, digging into her windpipe so she could hardly breathe. They met at the gate, and stood there calling one more time. 'Guzzler! Guzzler! Come home, boy!' but Lilac couldn't shout any more, and the heaving, gulping sobs she'd been keeping at bay finally came tumbling out instead.

CHAPTER 17

Lilac put down her pen and wriggled her fingers. Telling this story to Margery was hard work, because she didn't want to leave anything out. And because writing it down was almost like having it happen all over again. She blinked quickly a few times, swallowed hard, and went on with writing.

And then just when we were going to go inside we saw a car come really slowly down the road — at least, we saw its lights so the rest of the car was behind them — the way a car drives when someone's looking to see the numbers on the houses in the dark, which is impossible because the numbers are all up by the front doors or on the gate where you don't know to look, and somewhere different in each house and Mrs Malone's has a name instead of a number so you just have to go by the houses on either side.

And the car stopped and the driver rolled down her window and asked us if we were looking for a dog. She said she had found a hurt dog on the street near there and she took him to the vet but he had no tag on his collar and she didn't know who owned him. And then she'd come back to see if anyone was searching for him. I just kept crying and couldn't stop even though everything was probably okay and I was really happy inside but the outside of me hadn't got to that yet, and Mum sort of squeaked, and only Dad was able to answer her properly. And after they talked they said I had to go to bed because I'd had a big shock and Dad went off with the lady to the vet to see Guzzler and before they went she said he had a broken leg but he was fine and not dead at all.

I still had to go to school the next day, which is the most totally unfair thing of all because they wouldn't even let me go and see him at the vet's until after school and they said he was asleep so it didn't matter but of course it did and I was boiling with rage and then I got into trouble with Sr Joseph at music but she said 'Oh go on with you, child' and just stopped giving out to me even though I'm sure nobody told her that I had a REALLY GOOD REASON for not listening when she had said that the orchestra doesn't come in at that part.

I'm playing the recorder instead of singing now for the concert. I get to play the treble. It sounds lovely and woodeny even though it's plastic.

She had to stop there because somehow she had told the whole story even though she felt as if she had only given the barest bones of it. How could she explain what it feels like to fall asleep after so much crying that your body is all wrung out and empty, except that your heart is at peace because you know things are all right after all? Or how it felt to bury her face in Guzzler's shaggy fur and take a deep breath and know that he was still there? Or to wonder what would have happened if that lady hadn't stopped and found him and the next car along had just squashed him and if Lilac had then gone outside and found squashed Guzzler all over the road; and then she felt sick again just by imagining things that didn't even happen. There were a lot of feelings. She couldn't explain them all, she could only tell what had happened.

Lilac jumped off her bed and ran downstairs to Guzzler, who was sitting in state on the sofa, where he was never allowed. She needed his fur for a few minutes, just until the tears had backed down. He had a plaster cast on his leg so he couldn't go for walks yet, and they had to help him outside to the garden when he needed to go to the loo. Lilac had spent a long time telling him into his thick, dog-smelly coat what a terrible boy he was for running off and how awful it had been and how he must never ever do it again and how sad she was and how lucky they all were that the lady had found him. He nuzzled her neck in return and she knew that he was happy to be home and safe too.

*****

The morning after it all happened, the first thing Gerry had done was to go out and get the new tag for Guzzler's collar, even though the dog was still at the vet's and wouldn't be able to run anywhere for several weeks once he came home. And then he bought more fence to put over the top of the wall at the back of the house to keep Guzzler safely inside the garden. Lilac's mum said if Guzzler had any sense at all he'd know better than to run off ever again, and Lilac's dad said he didn't have a lot of faith in that dog's sense even before he probably gave himself concussion getting knocked down.

Gerry brought home a big puffy new dog bed too, which they were hoping Guzzler would like just as soon as he stopped being allowed sit on the sofa because he was a patient. He had been pretty quiet for the first day or two when he came home, but now he was starting to chew at his plaster cast and whine in the direction of the back door. Not to mention the trouble it was lifting him outside to do his business. Gerry said he could practically hear the discs slipping in his spine every time Guzzler needed a wee.

When she wasn't snuggling with Guzzler, who was growing fat on doggy treats and no exercise, Lilac had become once again fervent about the plight of the penguins. 'I think seeing an animal in distress really showed me that I have to help them,' she said to Agatha at school after she told her all about it.

'It was a message,' breathed Agatha, in awe. 'From the Great Beyond.'

'I don't think God is that mean, though. He wouldn't hurt Guzzler just to get me to notice the penguins. I'd already noticed them. I just mean that now I understand that I can't wait around for someone else to fix this. We have to try, Agatha, we really do.'

'We could advertise to get people to look for the Aquarium's lost sweepstakes ticket.' Lilac had told Agatha her dad's story about that.

'Or clean up that lady's office in case it's in there. It was pretty messy when she gave me her magazines for my project.'

'It probably got thrown in the bin years ago.'

'Well, the concert is going to make money. We just need to make sure people help the penguins with it.'

'Should we start a campaign?' Agatha asked. 'We could make signs saying 'Save the Penguins' and march up and down outside the Aquarium with them. And we could give ice cubes wrapped in newspaper to everyone queueing up to go inside, and tell them to drop them in the penguin habitat.'

'I could write a letter to Greenpeace!' said Lilac, inspired. Greenpeace were all over the news these days, and they cared about animals and the environment. Miss Grey was a big fan of Greenpeace, so Lilac and Agatha knew all about it.

Agatha didn't seem convinced that writing to such a far-off group would have any effect, but Lilac thought it was worth a try, especially if she used her best handwriting and fancy phrases. She'd had lots of practice writing letters to Margery; it was satisfying to have a chance to put her talents to good use.

That evening Lilac took out some of her nicest, and most grown-up-looking, fancy paper and wrote a heartrending description of the penguins' plight.

Dear Greenpeace,

I know you are busy with nuclear disarmourment and I agree that's definately important, but I thought you should also know about something happening in my very home town. We have an Aquarium where the penguins have no snow or ice or anything to keep them cold the way they should be for their proper habitat. I don't know how much longer they can last in these conditions. The Aquarium people are not penguin experts and I can't find one here anywhere to talk to about this.

I don't know where else to turn for aid. Greenpeace, you are the penguins' only hope. Please help them.

And then at the bottom of the page she signed her full name: 'Lilac Adelaide Philomena McCarthy'.

Most people started out with one middle name and then chose another for their Confirmation. But for reasons Lilac could never fathom, her parents had given her two middle names and one of them was the dreaded Philomena, which she hated even more than she hated Lilac. Next year when she made her Confirmation she would get another one and then her whole name would never fit on any forms ever.

She could have just left out the Philomena but she felt dishonest if she did that. On the other hand, she didn't want the Greenpeace people to think she'd already made her Confirmation because for one thing that would also be dishonest and for another she would never *choose* a name like Philomena, and she would hate anyone to think she had. She almost put a little note in to explain that at the bottom, but there wasn't enough space so she didn't.

The envelope that went with the paper had a red line around the border and a tiny drawing of Strawberry Shortcake on the back. Lilac didn't think Greenpeace would take her any less seriously for that, and it was important that they matched, so that was the one she used.

CHAPTER 18

It was time for a big rehearsal for the Aquarium-benefit Christmas concert. There would be no Duran Duran. Lilac was playing recorder in the orchestra and all the other schools were participating; and Sister Joseph was going just a little bit bonkers, as Katie Byrne put it, because she wanted the girls from Lilac's school to be absolutely positively the best-behaved and best-rehearsed performers, but the girls didn't seem to think that was as important as she did, she said.

On Tuesday morning instead of going to school, everyone involved in the concert had to be at the church at nine o'clock. Lilac felt strange locking her bike outside the church and walking through the church's back doors in her school uniform with her schoolbag on her back. As she walked up the side aisle inside, things looked even stranger, compared to the usual Sunday sight of quiet adult backs-of-heads. Sister Joseph in navy and white was trying to direct girls quietly with a lot of vigorous pointing, while on the other side Father Byrne was talking much louder than anyone else would dare to in a church as he told the boys exactly where to put their coats and bags before they sat in their appointed pews.

As she got nearer, Lilac realised that Sister Joseph was, in fact, talking as well as pointing, but her voice was mostly swallowed up and taken away by the tall arches of the ceiling. Lilac added her coat and bag to the mountainous pile in the corner and sat down at the end of a pew beside Katie, not wanting to cause trouble by trying to insert herself into the middle where Agatha already was.

After a few minutes of vacant gazing, she remembered that she was meant to be with the orchestra, so she had to get out of the pew again, scrabble in the pile to pull her recorder out of her bag, and find a free chair with a music stand in front of it. The musicians were grouped at the side of the altar. Two teenage boys with guitars were already there, as well as one younger boy sucking on a clarinet – or maybe it was an oboe. There were several of the big girls in the navy uniform and three in the wine uniform from the other school. One of them, Lilac realised with a start, was Jeannie, holding a violin. Lilac gave a little wave but Jeannie didn't see her. Maura Rooney and Lizzy McDonald from Lilac's class were sitting to one side, with their recorders. Another boy who looked vaguely familiar was brandishing a recorder at his classmates in the front pew, but he hadn't claimed a chair.

A music teacher from the older girls' school was in charge of the orchestra. 'You're a motley bunch, but you'll have to do,' was her opening comment as she stood on the broad step in front of them.

Her name was Mrs Brady. She wore a bright red jacket

with shoulder pads that made her look like an important businesswoman, and the blouse underneath had a little ruffle at the neck. Her lipstick matched her jacket exactly, and Lilac couldn't be sure whether she was being funny or mean. Her expression didn't give much away in either direction.

Sister Joseph came over with the music for the recorders, and everyone was busy for a few minutes with flurries of photocopied pages that wouldn't stand up on the music stands. Finally, by folding the paper lengthwise for rigidity and mangling a few paperclips, Lilac got hers to stay still enough to read from. Maura and Lizzy had grabbed one stand between them, and Lilac was left to share her music with the boy who had looked familiar. When he sat down, Lilac realised he was one of the Jennings boys from up the road. She looked up from under her hair and mumbled 'Hi', but he ignored her. She knew he had no idea who she was, and she didn't feel like explaining because she'd have to look at him to do that.

It was so long since she'd had a friend who was a boy, and she saw her cousins so rarely, that she wasn't quite sure how things worked between boys and girls any more. Some of the girls in the class, she knew, hung out with boys and even talked scandalously about kissing them, but Lilac didn't really believe that part.

She almost felt as if the wrong end of a magnet was pushing her away from David – or was it Michael? – beside her. He had turned sideways on his chair to make rude faces at his friends, so she could observe him safely now: short, reddish-brown, curly-ish hair; freckles; a small hole in one knee of his dark grey school trousers. His laces were flattened, frayed, and flapping.

Eventually, everyone was in their allotted places and the rehearsal began. There were some pieces by each school's choir, some by everyone together, a few solos, and one piece where the orchestra – or 'the ensemble', as they were being called now – played alone. They sounded pretty bad to Lilac, but it was hard to tell when you were in the thick of it. She'd have to ask Agatha later. Some of the soloists were good, especially one girl from Jeannie's school who was obviously the star performer, and the pieces where everyone sang sounded impressively booming with the deep, older boys' voices included. Lilac almost thought it wouldn't be total cheek to expect people to pay to listen to them, especially since it was for a good cause. And the best thing about having all the schools involved was that if everyone had two parents and maybe a granny or an auntie who pretty much had to come, then you had three multiplied by all those students, which should fill the church quite well.

Lilac was busy working out just how many people that might be, and wondering how many the church could hold, and how much they were going to charge for tickets, and how much the Aquarium needed anyway, when her stomach rumbled and she realised that it was probably lunchtime. Looking around, she saw the teachers tap their watches and nod at each other in agreement that everyone was tired and hungry and restless and that they should stop now for the time being and get back to proper classes. Father Byrne went up to the front of the church and announced that the rehearsal was over and students were to please exit quietly and reverently.

With a lot of kerfuffle, people found their coats and bags, clangily folded up music stands, lined up by the door, and left the church to its usual quiet weekday-morning routine. They had walked almost all the way to school when Lilac remembered that her bike was still locked up outside the church.

'Do you think if someone wanted to steal my bike, they could pop into confession first and be forgiven before they'd even done it?' she asked Katie Byrne, who was somehow beside her again. Katie giggled but didn't answer, and Lilac missed Margery, who liked any opportunity to do her parish priest impression.

CHAPTER 19

Dear Lilac,

Caroline says she's going to be a lespion. I don't know what a lespion is but Caroline says the boys at school are all so stupid that she'll have to be one. And then she said something about how the nuns are all lespions. But she hates going to mass so it's wierd that she wants to be anything that's like nuns. Maybe it's French, so it would be a l'Espion. I can't find it in the dictionary. I'm learning quite a lot of French cos the signs are all in English and French here, and all the things we buy in the shops have French writing on their boxes. In some places in Canada they speak French everywhere. I'm glad Dad came to the normal bit, though, even if it is colder than humanly possible. You would not believe how fat my new mittens are.

I was on the edge of my chair reading about when Guzzler went missing and I nearly cried when he was all right at the end. You should definatly do Author for your career project. Or is that over already? I got a B+ for my diorama in the end. I used lots of cottonwool balls to make snow but the teacher said there wasn't enough detail in my city scape. That's because when it snows you can't see anything. I was being realistic. I should have gone with my first idea which was to cover it all in black paper and say it was a city at night when there's a power cut.

You definitely have to save the penguins now, after Guzzler's traumatic episode. What can I do to help? Can I start a petition here? I'm sure I could get all my class to sign it. In the summer here they probably understand exactly how the penguins feel without their snow and ice.

Oh! I just had an idea. You said there's a place with artificial snow in Dublin where people can ski. You should bring the penguins there. Maybe even just for a holiday, to keep them going until their habitat gets fixed properly. That would help them remember what snow is like and make them happier.

Tell me if you find out what lespions are.

Many excellent tidings,

Margery

Lilac was as baffled as Margery about lespions, but the ski slope idea was a good one. Jeannie was coming to babysit, so she thought she could interrogate her about both things.

Jeannie had asked if she could bring a friend this evening. Lilac's mum had said yes, of course. After she put the phone down, she clucked.

'Oh. Oh, I hope it's not a *boy* friend.'

'Why not?'

'Because. They might get Up. To things. Unsupervised.'

'Oh. Right.' Kissing and such, Lilac supposed she meant. 'But I'll be here. I can supervise.'

'*You*'ll be going to bed, madam.'

But it was all right because when Jeannie appeared on the doorstep she was with another girl.

'This is Rachel', Jeannie said, and she and Rachel shuffled inside and put their coats in the right place.

'You play the flute', said Lilac. Rachel looked surprised and agreed that she did.

'I'm a recorder. A treble,' Lilac clarified. 'In the concert.'

'Oh yeah, sure.' A bit vaguely, though, as if she hadn't actually noticed there were any recorders sitting behind the much more important real-orchestra-instrument flutes.

Rachel had blonde hair that was short at the sides and long at the back, and her eyelashes were thick and black. She and Jeannie were both still in their school uniforms, though they had been wearing their anoraks over them instead of their school coats. Lilac was pretty sure Rachel's eyelashes hadn't been that black when she'd seen her at the rehearsal. Now that Lilac looked again at Jeannie, she appeared to have some green stuff under her eyes too, right inside the eyelid. It made her eyes look sort of sore but also a bit cool, like someone on *Top of the Pops*.

'Hello Jeannie, is this your friend?' said Lilac's mum with some relief, coming down the hall in high heels and a dark-red dress with a swirly paisley pattern. 'I hope you girls have brought some homework to do, since it's a school night. Gerry should be home before ten but I have to go out now, so just make sure that Lilac's in bed by nine, please.'

She put on her coat and wafted out the front door, waving a kiss in Lilac's direction.

Lilac had finished her homework and was watching a travel programme. Jeannie and Rachel didn't appear to have brought any schoolbooks. They settled in for *Eastenders*, which came next, and was exciting in parts, though quite scandalous. Lilac wasn't actually certain whether she was allowed to watch it or not, as she usually didn't.

Only half paying attention to Dirty Den's villainy, Rachel took a tube of mascara out of her bag and started to put more mascara on her lashes. Lilac watched with interest. She had always assumed that once you had mascara on, you were done, but Rachel evidently liked to reapply indefinitely, the more the better. Soon each set of eyelashes looked like an enormous half-spider sitting over her eye. Lilac kept expecting them to stick to Rachel's cheeks whenever she blinked, but they didn't.

Jeannie and Rachel kept making little comments to each other that Lilac couldn't really understand, and then giggling a lot because they were obviously terribly funny. Lilac wasn't as comfortable with this Jeannie as with the usual Jeannie-on-her-own: she couldn't talk to her, and she didn't like all those *Eastenders* people anyway. 'I'm going to go and write to Margery', she announced. 'I'll come back for *Fame*.'

Dear Margery,

Michael Jennings from up the road is playing recorder in the concert too. He's a bit younger than me, but he's in fifth class like us. He wasn't even playing properly for most of our part but the teacher couldn't tell. I don't think he knows that I know who he is. He's in the photo of my 4th birthday party, I looked at it last night to make sure. We're all in the back garden and he's wearing a pair of horrible red dungarees and his hair is long and really babyish. I don't think I ever went to his birthdays, though. When I was four my best friend was Anne O'Mahony. Isn't that funny, because now I hardly ever talk to her. I think we were just friends because our mums knew each other. They used to have coffee mornings and Anne and I would play. One day she wet her pants at my house and she had to go home with nothing on under her skirt and her pants in a plastic bag. There's a photo of us from that day too but I'm the only person who knows she has no knickers on in it.

It's time for Fame so I have to go.

Benevolent wishes,

Lilac

PS. Don't tell anyone that about Anne. It might be mean. She's quite nice, I just don't really like her now.

Usually Lilac liked to put on her old ballet leotard and a headband and legwarmers and dance around the room to the *Fame* songs, but tonight she decided not to. Jeannie and Rachel started singing along to the theme tune, though, and Lilac joined in, so it almost felt as though they were all friends.

At the first ad break Lilac decided the time was right. She addressed herself to the room in general.

'My friend Margery had a question and I said I'd ask you because you might know. What's a lespion? Have you ever heard of it? It might be something to do with Mass, or it might also be French. Do you do French?'

Jeannie and Rachel looked at each other and burst out laughing. Lilac didn't know what to do, so she just kept talking.

'It's just that Margery's sister said she's going to be one, but Margery didn't know what she meant . . .' A thought struck her. 'Do you know Margery's sister? Caroline Dillon? She went to your school before they moved to Canada.'

There was a pause in the two girls' hilarity. They looked at each other with eyes made huge with mock shock and said 'Oh – My – God' in unison, and then they giggled even harder. Lilac was lost and left behind again, but luckily the ads went away and Fame came back and that was the end of it. At the next ad break she watched intently as Maurice Pratt explained his low, low prices, and she tried not to pay any attention to all the significant looks and loud whispering going on between Jeannie and Rachel. She didn't feel it was the right time to bring up the ski slope and the penguins after all, now that the mood had changed.

111

When *Fame* ended, none of them sang the theme song. Lilac said goodnight and put herself to bed. For all I know, she thought grumpily as she wormed her way between chilly sheets, Jeannie and Rachel could be kissing *each other* downstairs *unsupervised*. That would give Mum a right shock.

CHAPTER 20

'They can't call it a dress rehearsal when we're not dressed up. We should have costumes.' Lilac was indignant.

Agatha, as usual, presented the voice of reason. 'But we are wearing what we'll be wearing for the concert, so we're dressed in the right things.'

'But it's our uniforms. We'd be wearing them today anyway. What'll be strange is wearing them on a Saturday night for the real concert. It should be called a reverse dress rehearsal. Or . . . something.'

Sometimes Lilac felt as if she was just arguing for the sake of it. When she used to argue with Margery it was fun because it felt like bouncing a ball back and forth between them. Arguing with Agatha was more like bouncing it on grass that made the ball bounce a little less each time. Agatha was nice, but did she have to always be so – well, so *right*?

This rehearsal was not so much about the clothes and more about running through all the pieces in the right order for the concert. Adele Duffy was not impressed with the fact that Agatha had been picked as a soloist and she hadn't.

'But I was a Billie Barry Kid, Sister Joseph.'

'Indeed, child, we are well aware of that fact. I need your nice strong voice in the choir to help everyone else along.'

Lilac nudged Agatha. 'That means she sings so loud that everyone has to help drown her out.'

'Agatha, you'll need to sit here at the end of the first row where you can easily slip out when it's your turn,' said Sister Joseph, pointing at a different pew. Agatha squeezed past everyone in the pew to move to her new place.

'And Lilac, why are you in the middle there? You know you need to be with the *ensemble*.' Sister Joseph always said 'on-som-bul' pointedly, as if she particularly disliked having to say a French word.

'But we don't play anything until after the first solos, Sister. I thought I was meant to be here.'

Sister Joseph gave Lilac one of her best withering looks and Lilac scrambled over all the legs and back out to the ensemble seats without further discussion. She was still sitting beside Michael, who once or twice had actually spoken to her now as they shared the treble recorder score. Mostly the trebles played the bass line with the other low instruments – there were two cellos and a bassoon from Jeannie's school – so they were generally not at all heard and it didn't make much difference whether they played or not. Maybe the audience would hear them all, but from where Lilac sat, the bassoon was loud enough to carry the whole bass line on its own. The flutes and the violins got all the best melodies, with the descant recorders joining in at the places where Sister Joseph decided they didn't sound too bad. Lilac was pretty sure they only had recorders at all so that the two primary schools could be represented in the instrumental group.

As they waited for Father Byrne to decide who was going next, Michael spoke to Lilac.

'You own that dog, don't you?' he said

Lilac was startled. 'Yes. Guzzler. You live at the end of my road.'

'I know. I see you go by all the time with him. I wish we had a dog.'

'Everyone should have a dog. Dogs are . . . great,' she finished lamely, because it was impossible to describe how important Guzzler was or how wrong it would feel not to have him.

'I remember one time when it was that really hot summer we rolled down the hill at the back of your garden and your dog kept trying to catch us because he thought we were all falling over.'

'I remember that too! Was that you? I thought it was my cousins. Dad says Guzzler's got no brain at all, but he's highly intelligent really. I think he's part sheepdog, that's why he wanted to rescue everyone.'

'My mum says she spent long enough getting the three of us toilet trained and she's not starting again with a creature who's never going to clear away his own dinner plate. I don't think it's fair. If we had a dog I'd clear his dinner plate away for him.'

'I think . . .' Lilac had to stop there because Mrs Brady was tapping her conductor's stick on her music stand for attention. It was time to look as if they were playing again.

As she played the succession of long low notes that went

along with this particular piece – just like every other piece – Lilac considered with surprise how normal a conversation that had been. She started thinking what she'd write to Margery about it, but then she remembered that Margery had a friend now who was a boy, and she probably talked to boys in a perfectly normal way all the time at school.

Agatha wasn't too happy about her solo, but her mum was involved in the arranging of the concert and was going to accompany her on violin, so she couldn't really get out of it. When it was time to rehearse Agatha's part, Lilac craned her neck to see who would be playing beside her, looking for the tall dramatic woman she'd imagined back at the start of the school year.

'What are you looking for?' whispered Michael, wondering why Lilac was bending backwards so far she might fall off her chair.

'That's my friend Agatha, going to sing next. I want to see her mum.'

'Why is her mum here?'

'Because she plays the violin. She's accompanying Agatha.'

She was still looking in vain for anyone with long reddish hair or flowing skirts when a petite woman with short black hair came through the doors from the side of the altar and went over to the podium where the soloists performed. Her movements were brisk and deft, and she wore a thin black polo-neck, slim-fitting black trousers, and bright red lipstick. Something about the part of her face where her nose met her mouth seemed familiar, though Lilac couldn't pin it down, exactly.

'Well, that can't be her,' Lilac observed to Michael. This woman was absolutely not the type to see auras or commune with nature at the top of a cliff. Lilac couldn't really remember which parts of her idea of Agatha's mum were entirely her own invention and which were things Agatha had really said.

Even so, this woman picked up a violin, murmured something to Agatha, nodded three times to count them both in, and began to play. After a few bars, Agatha's reedy voice rang through the church, surprisingly loud considering the microphone wasn't yet set up.

'She's OK,' said Michael.

Lilac was pretty sure she was better than that, but understood that boys couldn't ever be heard to make strong statements about things they liked, unless they involved football. She glowed a little with pride at being Agatha's friend.

CHAPTER 21

The week of the concert had finally arrived. It felt as if they'd been preparing for ever, but it was still a surprise, somehow, that the real thing was so close. Lilac didn't know what she'd do with her time when there were no special choir practices and no rehearsals in the church, and when school didn't include a nice walk there and back to break up the tedium of normal lessons.

It was fun, too, being in the church at odd times of day, not because you were at Mass or going to Confession, but on official business. Not being a customer, you might say, but like someone who worked there. Lilac loved being allowed into the sacristy, where they'd been a few times now, and seeing the priests and the altar boys behind the scenes, 'backstage'. The instruments were all being stored there so that nobody had to lug a cello back and forth.

On Thursday, Lilac had to go into the sacristy to pick up her recorder because she needed to practice her part at home – even though they were meant to know it all by now. There was one line of music in one particular piece where the audience could actually hear the treble recorders because only they and the violas were playing, so she really needed to get it right. She couldn't rely on Michael to even blow into his instrument, let alone put his fingers in the right places, so it was all up to her.

So after school she went home by the church, and feeling important (but still a bit nervous, even though she had every right to be there), knocked at the sacristy door at the side of the building. When nobody answered, she gingerly pushed open the heavy wooden door and looked in. The sacristy was a large rectangular room, the whole centre of which was taken up with random pieces of dark wooden furniture of varying heights, and there were shelves and tables and cabinets of various sorts all around the walls, leaving just a narrow passsage between them all that you could walk through to get to the part of the room you needed to be in, and from there to the connecting door into the church itself.

Lilac couldn't see anyone there, so she walked in quietly and respectfully – because even though it wasn't quite the church, it was still a place you had to be fairly holy – and went over to where the instruments were. It should have taken no more than a second to pick her recorder off the top of the pile of instrument cases, but its bottom edge was jammed under a folded-up music stand with all the sheet music piled on top of it. She had to carefully lever up the messy stack of pages before she could pull her instrument out. With a sharp tug she jerked it free – only to discover that it was the one thing the whole pile had been balancing on. Everything collapsed in a deafening clatter of music stands and violin cases and a swathe of falling paper.

'Jaysus!' A loud exclamation came from the far corner of the room and Lilac swung around to see who was there. As she did, the recorder she was now holding swung with her, and knocked over a small cardboard box on her other side. Little white discs scattered all over the floor, like pieces out of a giant's paper-hole punch, or tiny frisbees.

'Is that . . . ?' she began. And then, '. . . Oh NO!'

Lilac stood fixed to the spot. She was pretty certain those inch-wide white discs were Holy Communion wafers, and she was also absolutely definitely sure that knocking about a hundred of them onto the grubby carpet with a treble recorder was probaby a mortal sin that would get her excommunicated, or at least sent to sit at the back of the church saying the entire rosary five times a day for months and months. She was out of the concert, that was certain. She was afraid to even try to pick them up, because probably putting her unholy germs on them would make things even worse.

She looked up slowly to see whose shout it was that had made all this happen. Father Byrne. Of course. He was holding something in his hand that Lilac vaguely noticed looked like a paintbrush, though for some reason it made her think of her mum rather than her dad. He had been standing in front of the mirror that was in one corner of the room, presumably put there so a priest could check he didn't have any spinach stuck between his teeth before he went out to say Mass, but there was a tall wooden stand with a long hanging banner from Easter on it right between Lilac and that part of the room, so she hadn't seen him. Now, though, he was striding towards her, only to stop short at the outermost discs that were scattered in a perfect circle around their box.

'Where did you spring from? What are you doing?' He looked at the brush in his hand, as if only now realising he still held it, and quickly put it down on the nearest surface. His eyes took in the scene of disaster before him, starting with the tangle of music stands and instrument cases behind Lilac and ending up with the white dots on the carpet. Close to, the 'glow' that people always remarked on was more obvious – sort of orange and sparkly, Lilac thought. Maybe when a priest was about to excommunicate someone they got all tingly and bright. She wondered if he'd have to point a sceptre at her, or a sword, maybe, and speak in a voice that came directly from the Pope, as if he had a poltergeist inside him. No, not a poltergeist. One of those other ones.

But instead of pointing anything at her, even a finger, the priest nimbly knelt down and started to collect the Communion wafers, saying, 'No harm done, help me pick these up before someone stands on them. Mrs O'Connor hoovered in here this morning, so I'm sure it'll be fine. Just maybe don't mention it to Sister Joseph. Or any of the congregation, perhaps. Or your friends at school. Let's keep it between us, eh? *All* of it,' he ended meaningfully; though Lilac wasn't quite sure what else he could be talking about.

After they'd put all the wafers back in their box, Father Byrne helped Lilac put the music stands back in the corner. 'They were certainly precarious, balanced up there, weren't they? And all that sheet music should really be in a folder or something. Sure, it'd blow away if anyone opened a window.'

Lilac didn't say a word. She was afraid to break whatever spell it was that was stopping the priest from being very very angry. He still looked dark and glittery, but he didn't sound even a little bit annoyed. When everything was tidy, she stuffed the recorder into her schoolbag and left, without even saying goodbye or sorry Father, or anything polite at all.

Dear Margery

I knocked over a big box of communion in the sacristy when I went to get my recorder. Fr Byrne was there and I thought he was going to KILL me but he didn't. He didn't even make me go to confession or anything. Now I'm thinking about it though, he didn't say that God forgives me. Maybe he's going to let God punish me. Maybe that's why he never gave out to me.

If something terrible happens to me, you'll know that it was God punishing me. He also said not to tell anyone about it, but you don't count because you're not here. Do you think God will punish me more for telling you when he said not to? But I didn't promise. I might have nodded, but you can't be sure someone's promising if they look like they're nodding. Maybe I was just trying to scratch my nose on my scarf, not nodding at all.

I'm mostly joking, don't worry. But just in case.

Also, I think Father Byrne wears bronzer. It's not a holy glow at all. If God punishes me and I die horribly, you can tell everyone that to get my revenge because Father Byrne should have just forgiven me properly.

The concert is on Saturday. I hope Michael doesn't mess up the treble line because Father Byrne will probably think that's my fault too.

Love
from
Lilac
in
probably
eternal
damnation

CHAPTER 22

Saturday came. Lilac hung around all day doing basically nothing, saving her energy for the big event. The concert began at five in the afternoon. An odd time for something to start, her mother said, just when everyone was starting to get hungry. Gerry wanted to know if they would be selling packets of crisps and popcorn and those little ice creams in tubs with wooden spoons in the lids in the interval to ruin everyone's dinners but create even more revenue. Lilac hadn't heard about any such plans and couldn't really imagine the audience tucking into ice creams and crinkling crisp bags in church, even if it wasn't Mass. Someone would have to sweep up all the rubbish, and sweeping in between the pews and the kneelers would be an awful job, never mind any sticky spots where small children might drip their ice cream.

Eventually the time came to put on her school uniform – how strange, on a Saturday afternoon – with a freshly ironed blouse even though it was all hidden under the pinafore, and the black shoes she had polished herself, and her whitest knee-socks pulled up as high as they would go, which was not as far as her knees. She must have grown since the last time she'd needed them, as she'd been wearing grey tights to school since the start of November.

As an important soloist-or-member-of-the-ensemble, Lilac had to be at the church a whole half-hour before the concert was due to start.

'I can't walk there, Mum, it might rain and my uniform would get all messed up. And smelly. You know how uniforms are smelly when they're wet.'

'Ah, the nostalgic aroma of wet wool,' her mother mused, winding a bright red scarf around her neck. 'All right, we'll all go early. Gerry, are you ready?'

'I'm as ready as I'm going to get. I don't have to wear a tie, do I? We won't even be taking off our coats, the church is always Baltic.' Lilac's dad jingled the car keys in his pocket to make sure they were there, and put on his warm brown hat with the brim, as well as his big coat. He looked like an American detective, Lilac always thought, though he really needed to be smoking to pull it off, and she was glad he didn't smoke. Lilac kissed Guzzler goodbye and brushed Guzzler hairs off her uniform skirt.

'Anyway, we'll get a good parking spot,' Gerry said mostly to himself, as he backed the car carefully out of the driveway.

He parked right beside the door to the church, where Lilac wasn't convinced there was even a space.

'It's fine, Lilac, it's dark, that's all, you can't see the lines. I know there's a space here, sure I've seen it many a time and coveted it because that big navy Merc is always taking it.'

'Now, Lilac, whose mother am I going to meet?' asked Nuala as they started to go in. 'You need to warn me or I'll forget who's who. Oh, there are the Jenningses, look how big the oldest one is getting now . . .'

'Mum, I told you, Michael Jennings is playing treble beside me.'

'Did you? Oh yes, so you did. And of course Eileen said she'd see me here because her Jeannie's singing a solo, was that it?'

'Mum, do you listen to anything? She's a violin.'

'Yes, yes . . .' Her mother was going into social-butterfly mode, ready to meet and greet happily and laugh at other people's ordinary remarks in a way that made them feel witty and entertaining. Gerry looked somehow taller than usual, and imposing (maybe it was the hat), and Lilac felt just a little bit proud of them. They were, tonight at least, not terrible parents to have in front of everyone else from school. So long as they didn't say anything embarassing, at least they looked all right. She muttered a quick 'See you after', and peeled away from them to collect her music and get set up.

Everything worked the way it was supposed to. The soloists sounded lovely. The choir sounded pretty good. Even the ensemble, Lilac thought from her acoustically hampered position, was probably okay. Nobody's clarinet squawked at a quiet bit and nobody's violin screeched in the wrong direction. The treble recorders played their parts admirably, and on the line where it was just themselves and the viola, she and Michael played out confidently and a little line of invisible connection ran between them because they were so perfectly in unison. They exchanged a happy grin of relief when that particular piece was over, and Lilac snuck a look at the audience to see her mother and Mrs Jennings sharing a similar smile.

Father Byrne, announcing each piece, looked as if he was just back from three weeks in Jamaica, but all the old ladies in the audience probably just talked about his lovely healthy glow and how radiantly holy he was.

Lilac was on a high when the last round of applause was done and the performers were finally released into the audience to gabble and preen at their family members. Mothers were chatting to each other and fathers were putting on scarves and wondering how soon they could get out of this melée and off home.

'Did you see me in the third piece when I nearly dropped my recorder? And did you notice the girl with the blonde plaits in the choir who walked up the centre aisle when it was time for her solo? That was Jenny and she was meant to go round the side but she messed up and Sister Joseph was fuming but she couldn't say anything . . .'

'Jenny who, Lilac? Everyone's just Jenny this and Mary that these days – I might know her mother at the tennis club if you'd only say her last name.'

'Mum, you don't know her mother. Jenny O'Herlihy. And there's nobody called Mary. That's a totally old-fashioned name. Did you like the duet? Did it sound good? Wasn't Agatha's solo lovely?'

Indeed it was. I should go and congratulate Mrs Kovac, actually. I met her at the community meeting when they were planning the concert, but I didn't realise she was your Agatha's mum. Because you didn't say her last name, you see. She's the treasurer of the committee, as well as being an accomplished violinist.'

'Fine, fine.' Lilac was suddenly exhausted. She wanted to be at home with just Guzzler.

'I'm going to wait in the car. Dad, can I have the keys?'

'I'll come with you, Lilac. It's high time we were off, I'm not sure I parked in a proper parking space at all and we might be holding up the troops.'

'But Gerry, you said . . .' Nuala was exasperated. 'Oh, all right, we'll all go.'

Lilac tumbled into bed no more than twenty minutes later, too exhausted to even brush her teeth and hoping her dentist would give her a pass, just this once. She'd seen her dentist at the concert, actually. It seemed like everyone she knew had been there, and a lot more people besides. The evening had been a roaring success, everyone said – and she fell asleep thinking of happy penguins who would soon cavort in a new frozen wonderland of their very own. There would be no need to resort to wild schemes of kidnapping and ski slopes.

CHAPTER 23

Dear Lilac,

Did God smite you yet for dropping all the holy communion? If there's any thunder and lightning you should probably stay indoors, but even then it might strike the chimney pot and come down and get you on the sofa. You should probably just stay in bed, but then you'd miss the concert.

I suppose the concert will be over by the time you get this. Especially since it was already over by the time I got your letter. So first you'll have to go back in time and then you'll have to avoid the lightning. If you've already been struck by lightning it's too late.

Anyway, I asked Mum about communion without saying it was you who knocked some over, and she said that if it hasn't been confiscated then it's not holy yet. At least, I think that's what she said. So maybe it wasn't holy yet and it's OK.

I discovered that when people say hockey here they always mean ice hockey. We went to see an ice hockey game and it was majorly dangerous and exciting. The players kept ignoring the ball thingy and just having fights and every now and then they'd slam against the plastic glass at the side of the ice because they were going so fast and it would all shake like mad. One team won but I wasn't paying attention to who it was. There was a lot of shouting.

Caroline got a letter from one of her friends at school and now she says she never wants to go back to Ireland at all. She's going to stay in Canada for ever, which is good for now because she's not going to try to run away any more, but it might be difficult next summer when it's time to go home. In the letter her friend said that everyone in school is saying that Caroline's a lezzer. Caroline's really angry because she says she had a boyfriend before anyone else in her class (I think that's true) and that she nearly got pregnant last year (I didn't know that) and she can't understand where a rumour like that would come from. But there was this one girl who wanted to go out with Danny and she thinks it's her. Only she used more swear words when she was telling me but I won't put those in because I'm ladylike and refined.

I hope the concert went well and you're not horribly dead.

Love Margery

There were some times when Lilac really noticed the difference that having a big sister made between her and Margery. Margery knew all the swear words, for one thing, though she said she chose not to use them except in emergencies. And even though Lilac had heard some of the girls at school accuse each other of being lezzers, she was pretty hazy on what it actually meant. It seemed to work as a general all-purpose insult, mostly. 'You big lezzer!' Theresa Quirke had shouted at Laura Devine when Laura broke her ruler one morning before Miss Grey had arrived. 'I am not!' Laura retorted, mightily offended.

There were no 'lez–' words at all even in the giant dictionary on Lilac's mum's shelf, the one where she looked up words from books if she was feeling particularly curious or self-educational. And Lilac had no intention of asking Jeannie anything ever again, even if she came on her own next time. But if it had something to do with getting pregnant – well, that must be very serious.

There were so many words in the world, just in English, Lilac sometimes wondered how she was ever going to learn them all. And they had to start French in secondary school the year after next, so they'd be expected to know all of English by then, obviously.

CHAPTER 24

Agatha rushed into the classroom early on Monday morning, all of a tizzy. She dropped her bag, grabbed Lilac by the elbow, and said 'Quick! Come outside! I have to tell you something!'

Lilac usually squeaked into school at a minute past nine, just after Miss Grey had started to say the morning Hail Mary, but today she had arrived in good time and Miss Grey wasn't even at her desk yet. She went back out the door with Agatha, agog to find out what all the fuss was about.

Agatha took her around the corner towards the toilets, and insisted on looking up and down the deserted corridor like a spy before she would say a word. Then she whispered: 'Something terrible's happened!'

'I could have guessed that,' said Lilac. 'But what is it?'

'You know my mum was in charge of the money for the concert?'

'Was she? OK.' Lilac hadn't known that was what treasurer meant, but it made sense, since being an actuary had turned out to be a job to do with money, a bit like an accountant.

'So when the concert was over, Father Byrne said Mum should leave the money in the sacristy overnight, because that would be the safest place for it. So she put it all in the locked cash box and left that in the sacristy and Father Byrne locked the door behind him.'

'Right.' Lilac nodded along encouragingly. They heard Miss Grey's high heels start up the stairs below them, but then there was a whoosh of dropped papers and a gentle 'Oh dear' and the footsteps paused. 'Hurry up, we'll have to go in!'

'And yesterday morning when she went to pick up the money –' she paused dramatically '– it was gone!'

'What do you mean, gone?'

'Gone! Gone, gone! And so was Father Byrne!'

'He ran off with the money?'

'Yes! At least, that's what it looks like. It's a secret, I'm not meant to tell you.'

Miss Grey's heels started up the stairs again. Lilac and Agatha ran ahead of her back to the classroom and sat at their desks in the nick of time.

Lilac spent the rest of the morning dramatically wrinkling her brow and dropping her jaw at Agatha, who nodded vigorously in return. At break time they took their snacks to the farthest end of the playground and huddled in a sheltered corner beside the bike sheds where Lilac could finally let her questions flood out.

'But where did Father Byrne go? Did they tell the Guards? Do they really think he *stole* it? Maybe he just borrowed it. For an operation for a poor family's father . . . '

'They called the Gardaí once they realised that he was missing too, because he didn't show up to say the nine o'clock mass. He said the vigil mass after the concert, so he was the last one out – and then he disappeared.' Agatha said it with relish. She was quite enjoying being the one with the exciting story for a change.

'Your mum's not in trouble, is she?'

'No, it's not her fault. She did everything right and other people were watching. And he was on the committee too, so of course she trusted him.'

'And he's a priest.'

'Maybe he was just posing as a priest to steal the money.'

'He's been here for years, though. And working at the boys' school too. I don't think he'd have known that there was going to be a concert for the Aquarium . . .' she stopped, thinking through the consequences of all this for the first time. 'But wait. We did all that work and went to all the trouble of putting on the concert for nothing? If they don't get the money back, the Aquarium won't get anything! And the penguins will be trapped in their dusty non-snowy habitat for ever!'

'Sister Joseph's going to be pretty angry.'

Lilac grinned at the thought of Sister Joseph apoplectic with rage. 'If they do catch him, I'd say he'd rather go to prison than face her.'

'That's for sure.'

'We'd better go in, it's nearly time.' They ambled slowly towards the building, as if pulled by an invisible string; and then the bell rang and they moved a little faster.

Lilac and Agatha didn't say a word, but by the time Lilac

got home the news was already all over town. Her dad was first to greet her when she came through the door.

'Did you hear the news?' he said, rubbing his hands with the anticipation of a good story to tell to an avid audience.

'About Father Byrne disappearing with the concert money?'

'Oh, you did then.' He looked a bit deflated.

'Go on, tell me what you heard,' Lilac said, to cheer him up. And because he probably had a different version from hers.

'Well, apparently it's a good five thousand pounds, because as well as the proceeds from the concert, he made off with the poor-box money too. And they think he went to Spain. Or maybe Florida. Somewhere he can blend in, with that tan of his, I suppose.'

'It's not a tan, it's bronzer,' said Lilac, feeling that she didn't have to keep that particular secret any more.

'It is? Oh, well that explains that, then,' said Gerry. He paused. 'I always thought that fellow was a bit oily, didn't you?'

'Yes,' said Lilac, 'but everyone else said I shouldn't say that about a priest.'

CHAPTER 25

Father Byrne's misdeeds were all over the news in a few days' time, but he and his loot had managed to disappear quite effectively. With all their newfound spare time, and spurred on by anger at the waste of everyone's efforts raising all that money, Lilac and Agatha were redoubling their efforts to sort out the problem of the penguins.

'Margery thinks we should bring the penguins to the ski slope for a holiday. How could we do that?' Lilac said while they ate sandwiches at their desks during a rainy lunchtime.

She could tell that Agatha was having visions of all the penguins on a little penguin bus, with scarves round their necks and toting little penguin suitcases, waving bye-bye to the Aquarium staff and heading off for a rest cure in the Dublin mountains.

'*Realistically*, though,' she added, to bring Agatha back to earth.

'Well, maybe we could smuggle them out one by one instead of taking them all at once.'

'Hmmm.'

'And tell our parents that we wanted to find out about ski lessons so that they'd drive us up there, and then we could let the penguin out to play around on the snow –'

'– the artificial snow –'

'Well, what's artificial snow made of? It must be something cold and slippy, at least.'

'And then we'd bring that one back after a while and put it back into the Aquarium, where they wouldn't even have missed just one of them . . .'

'And it would tell all the other penguins about the lovely time it had, and give them hope for a better future . . .' Agatha was a hopeless romantic.

'And then do it again the next week with a lift from the other parent?'

'And then get them to sign us up for lessons, maybe, so we could take out a different penguin every week!'

'They're not library books, Agatha.'

'I *know*. We'd be a – a – penguin rehabilitation society. We might even become a registered charity, after a while, when they saw how happy it made the penguins. Then we could get the ski lessons for free, maybe.'

Lilac couldn't help thinking Agatha's imagination was running away with her. Being so closely involved with the Father Byrne drama must have gone to her head. Still, they had no options left. Greenpeace hadn't written back. The Aquarium couldn't afford to fix anything. The penguins had nobody else to look out for them.

On Friday after school, Lilac and Agatha went to the Aquarium again. Lilac approached the window feeling confident. The same woman as before looked up and raised her eyebrows a fraction to indicate that she was ready for Lilac to say something.

'Can me and my friend go in for a few minutes? Please? We've got 50p each. We're doing a project.' Projects were the perfect excuse for everything.

'You know we're closing in five minutes. You can go in, I suppose.' The woman heaved a sigh of put-upon-ness, took their coins, and churned out two pink tickets stuck together.

'Thank you!' said Agatha brightly. Honestly, Lilac would have expected Agatha to be a bundle of nerves on this slightly criminal expedition, but she looked excited and happy.

They pushed the heavy doors open and stopped for a moment to catch their breath and look at each other.

'Are we going to do this?'

'Yes! My Dad is ready to drive us to the ski slope before dinner. I said we just wanted to see it and pick up some information about lessons. Where are the penguins from here? We came in the other door with the school trip.'

Lilac pointed the way. They got to the penguin enclosure. There were no other visitors in sight, just like the last time Lilac had been there. The low wall was taller than all the penguins, but low enough for people to look over – or even to reach over.

'Which one?' said Agatha in a low voice.

Lilac surveyed the birds. As usual, they were loitering in small groups, looking like fat waiters waiting for the dinner rush to start. As she looked at them, the reality of what she and Agatha were proposing to do began to set in – how would they ever get a real live penguin out of the building and into Agatha's dad's car – and back again – without anyone noticing? Not to mention letting it enjoy the wilderness of fake snow at the ski slope without losing it? They should have brought Guzzler's spare collar and lead, if you could even put a collar on a penguin. When they'd been planning this, she was thinking of the penguins as fluffy, docile creatures, much like soft toys. Looking at the real thing, she could see that was a long way from the truth.

Agatha leaned over the low wall and reached down into the penguin area, holding out something small and brown and wiggling it at the nearest penguin.

'What's that?' Lilac said. It looked like a worm, and had already attracted the attention of the bird, who was advancing on Agatha's fingers with enthusiasm.

'It's an anchovy. My mum has a jar of them. They're tiny fish.'

'Really?' Lilac had to stop to take that in, even in the midst of this crisis. 'I thought anchovies were vegetables.'

'No, they're fish. Smell it.' Agatha swooped the fish away from the penguin, who had almost reached it, and held it towards Lilac's face.

'No, no, it's fine, I believe you. But Agatha –' Lilac began, as Agatha reached down and made a grab for the penguin, who was still following the sharp fishy smell of the anchovy, '– wait, don't . . .'

Agatha tried to pick him up, but he was heavier than she'd anticipated – he was taller than knee height, after all, and solid muscle and flesh under his feathers, not stuffing and foam. She almost overbalanced, the penguin emitted a loud squawk, and it tried to peck at her arm to defend itself. Agatha grabbed harder, firmly resolved.

'Stop that at once! What are you doing?' A sharp shout came from the other side of the large room, and fluffy, matronly Susan O'Sullivan emerged from the shadows, frantically batting Agatha away from the penguins' wall and sounding extremely cross.

*****

'But Lilac, I don't understand what Agatha was doing. Or why you were there in the first place. What is this obsession with the penguins?'

'Mum, please just stop. We've said we're sorry. We weren't trying to hurt the penguins, we were trying to help them. The only animal that suffered was the anchovy, and it was already dead.'

Lilac's mum didn't even bother to ask what anchovy Lilac was talking about. Lilac hadn't seen her this angry in a long time, not since Jimmy Jennings broke a window with his football and tried to put the blame on his visiting friend.

'Well, you're both barred from the Aquarium now, though I suppose since there's no money to fix it any more, it will just fall into disrepair and have to close. And then who knows where those poor penguins will go. But right now, they *have* a safe home, Lilac. I must say I don't know what to make of you two. It's most unlike you.'

She paused for breath. 'I suppose I have to put it down to the trauma of Guzzler's accident, and the shock of Father Byrne.'

'Yes, that's probably it.' Lilac went upstairs, feeling the

injustice of the world heavy on her shoulders, to write it all into a letter to Margery that she would post just as soon as she was ever allowed out of the house again.

CHAPTER 26

Dear Margery,

We're having a sponsored walk. We're just doing one for our class, because Miss Grey wanted to take us on an end-of-term trip, but she wasn't allowed, and then she wanted to take us on a hike, but she wasn't allowed, so then she called it a sponsored walk and the school had to let us do it. And now that all the money from the concert is gone, she said we could try to raise at least a little bit instead. I went along the road to ask the neighbours to sponsor me and when I got to Mrs Jennings she gave me 50p and said maybe the boys' school would do it too. The boys' school feels extra bad about it all because Father Byrne was their priest, so they want to make amends. Even though of course it's not their fault he turned out to be a dirty rotten low-down scoundrel.

So next Tuesday which is the day before the last day before Christmas holidays, we're going to walk up the hill and all the way around and back again, and Miss Grey says even if there's a hurricaine we'll still do it because the aquarium needs our support. Dad says if there's a hurricaine we'll all be blown into the sea and we'll all be exhibits for the aquarium instead.

I want to bring Guzzler because he's finally better enough to walk the whole way. I wonder could I get Mum to meet us there so that he could come too. Maybe I could get him his own sponsorship card.

Love from Lilac The Walker (don't worry you don't have to sponsor me. You don't even have proper money there, do you?)

Tuesday morning dawned clear and breezy, with no hint of a hurricane. It was a perfect day for walking. Friday would be Christmas Day, and Lilac's presents were almost ready – she had knitted things for her parents and for Guzzler, and was planning to decorate a shopping-list notebook for Granny, who would be coming up from Cork on Thursday morning. Christmas tests were mostly over and Lilac was pretty sure she hadn't failed anything, though some of the maths answers had just been guesses and her countries of Africa were a bit muddled over on the left where it bulged out. Lilac had that good sort of feeling you have when there are only nice things left to happen, and nothing nasty to get out of the way first – even if getting barred from the Aquarium was not exactly how she'd planned on ending her year.

'MUM!'

'Darling, I'm right here, there's no need to shout.'

'Oh, sorry, I thought you were upstairs.' Lilac turned around. 'So you're definitely going to bring Guzzler for a walk at ten o'clock, right? And we'll be coming along the road to the hill and you can just join in? I didn't ex*act*ly ask Miss Grey if it'd be all right, but I know it will.'

'I will, I will, don't worry.' Her mother was finally between books, just for now, which would last until lunch with the publishers sent her home to start making notes for the next one. She was taking lots of long blowy walks to clear her head of the last set of characters, she said, because they were still talking to her. Lilac knew that if someone else's mum was hearing voices in her head she'd be a bit worried, but this was how her mum always was. It was all right to hear voices so long as you wrote them down and called it a book, then everyone just said how clever you were.

Lilac thought it was silly to ride her bike to school just so that they could all turn around and walk back practically past her house again, but she did it anyway. They left school at nine-fifteen on the dot, walking in twos and threes behind Miss Grey and Sister Joseph, who had said she needed some fresh air. Lilac thought Sister Joseph missed being retired from a class teacher to only the sometimes music teacher this year.

Agatha was at the front because she wanted to hold the collection bucket, and Lilac was walking with Jenny

O'Herlihy. Jenny O wasn't bad, really; she was actually funny quite often, not like Jenny Kelly who giggled at nothing all the time. It was nice not having to walk on her own and look as if she didn't mind and was busy paying attention to other things instead. She would definitely have minded. They were going to meet the boys, who were walking with their teacher to the end of the main street, so they could all join up for the rest of the walk. The girls had signs saying 'Sponsored Walk' and 'In aid of the Aquarium' so that people might give them some extra money along the way. Lilac's sign said 'Save the Penguins', but Miss Grey hadn't noticed it yet.

From quite far off, the girls could see the group of boys all standing outside Byrne's Hardware waiting for them, as arranged. It occurred to Lilac for the first time to wonder if Father Byrne could possibly be related to Mr Byrne of the hardware shop, but she decided probably not. There were lots of Byrnes, all over the place. She wouldn't pop in to ask Mr Byrne if he knew where Father Byrne might have absconded to, then.

'Ladies first,' the boys' teacher said pleasantly when Miss Grey reached them, and all the girls walked past his smaller group before the boys fell into line at the end and started walking too. Lilac saw Michael as she went by and said hi, feeling a little self-conscious in front of his schoolfriends. He turned pink, and she hoped they weren't going to tease him about her now. They passed the church on the other side of the road, got to the top of the hill, and turned left down Lilac's street. Lilac was prancing just a little, because she wanted to be sure everyone knew which one was her house, and also because she hoped her plan about Guzzler would work out.

'This is my road!' she said loudly to Jenny. 'I wonder if I'll see anyone I know.'

They walked past Michael's house, but there was nobody at home and nothing to see there. Then Lilac saw her mum at the doorstep, wrestling an excited Guzzler onto his lead, and suddenly she wasn't sure that it had been a good idea. Nobody else's mum had come, after all. But from the back of the snake of girls Lilac could see her mother put on a look of surprise, as if she'd forgotten all about the walk and hadn't been pestered all week to sponsor anyone, and as if she'd love the chance to walk along with Miss Grey and hear all about her wedding plans. That was plenty for now, Lilac decided; when they got further up the hill she could take Guzzler's lead or maybe even let him off for a bit of a run around.

Agatha dropped back through the ranks to join up with Lilac and Jenny. 'Because the dog is up there now,' she said to them. 'I'm sure he's nice but I don't want to get too close, he just makes me nervous. Anyway, we're not going to pass many people who might give us money and the bucket was getting a bit heavy. I gave it to Theresa Quirke. Sister Joseph said it would keep her out of trouble to have a job to do. My mum said she might meet us up the hill too.'

Lilac was relieved that someone else had invited their mother, though really she had invited Guzzler, and her mum was just the person bringing him. 'Does Sister Joseph think Theresa's going to be talking to the boys?' Jenny wondered. Nuns were always extra concerned about talking to boys and that it would be a bad habit to get into.

Boys were sometimes known to smoke cigarettes or skip Mass.

'I'd be more worried that the boys might talk to Theresa,' said Lilac. 'If anyone's going to get you into bad habits like skipping Mass, I'd say it'd be her. I heard she smoked a whole cigarette once.'

'No, she didn't', said Jenny. 'She lives on my road and my big brother was there. He said she took half a puff and coughed up her lungs and swore to never ever touch a cigarette again. She'll even tell you herself. She's totally anti-smoking now.'

'Oh. Well, that's good. Not the lung thing, but the rest.'

The road turned up to the head, the big hump of land that jutted out at the end of the bay, curving around a little to make the strand sweep nicely at the bottom of the cliffs. They all knew this walk well: most of them had been pushed up it in prams before they could walk, and then been dragged up it whining about aching legs when they were too big to be pushed but not big enough to really walk the whole distance, and then probably been piggybacked part of the way by a sympathetic aunt or granddad before running down the gentle grassy slopes on the other side.

The side facing the sea, with the cliffs, was fenced off, and everyone knew that there was no playing around over there. That precipice was not to be toyed with. The slope might look gentle in some places, but then the hill would just drop away, eroded underneath by the world's lifetime of waves. Everyone's parents had told them a story – possibly not a true story, but some sort of story – of a little boy or girl who had run too far and gone over the edge.

As they left the town behind, the snake of two-by-twos

and three-by-threes had spread out and mingled. There was more room to walk in little clusters with bigger spaces between them, and by the time they got to the top of the head, the adults were in the middle with children ranging around them like spokes from a wheel. 'You can run around for a while,' the boys' teacher – Mr O'Grady was his name – shouted. It was windy up here and his voice carried much better than Miss Grey's would have done. Lilac took Guzzler from her mother and, telling him quietly to stay with her like a good boy, let him off the lead so he could gambol a little bit. Boys were mingling with girls, and vice versa, and Sister Joseph didn't appear to be panicking about it. Michael and his friend came over shyly to pet the dog.

'Hi,' he said to Lilac. 'I heard you were trying to rescue the penguins.'

'Where did you hear that?'

'My godmother told my mum. She works at the Aquarium.'

'Your mum does?'

'No, my godmother. We call her Aunty Sue but she's not really my aunty.'

'Well, I was trying to,' Lilac said defiantly. Michael was going to laugh at her now. 'They need to be in cold and ice and snow, not like that. And now the money's gone they'll never be saved.'

'They don't, actually.'

'What?'

'They're Humboldt penguins. They live in warmer areas, not the Antarctic, so they don't need to be in ice and snow.'

'How do you know?'

'Because after you and your friend were there, Aunty Sue looked properly at the sign and saw that it was wrong. It had been there for so long that nobody had noticed it for years.'

Lilac blinked at Michael in surprise. 'Humboldt? You mean where it said "The humble penguin" it was meant to say "The Humboldt penguin"?'

'That's right. That's what she told my mum. I think she felt a bit guilty about it, since she's the penguin expert and all.'

'Marine biologist,' Lilac corrected him, as she looked around for Agatha to tell her this astounding news. She felt as if some sort of small weight had been lifted off her chest, hearing that the penguins were quite all right, and being able to lay the blame for the whole thing at the foot of some anonymous incompetent sign-maker of the past.

While Lilac and Michael were chatting, Agatha had been keeping her distance from Guzzler, looking out to sea. She spotted something just by the fence, and wanted to get closer to find out what it was. Being a recent import to the town, Agatha had not been pushed up the hill as an infant and constantly warned away from the cliff as a toddler. Miss Grey had told everyone to stay well back from the edge this morning, but Agatha had been sorting out her sign and her collection bucket just then, so she hadn't really paid attention.

CHAPTER 27

Without warning, Guzzler broke away from Lilac's side and ran for the cliffs.

'Guzzler! Bad dog! Come back!' Lilac shouted, but her words were whipped away by the wind.

Time slowed to a crawl as a lot of things happened at once, but Lilac could do nothing except stand and watch, as if it was a film clip that had to play out to the end. She saw Guzzler race to where Agatha was leaning with all her weight on the rusty fence, reaching towards the grass on the other side of it for something just beyond her grasp. At the moment the dog reached her, the fence gave way, the ground under Agatha's feet started to crumble, and Agatha began to lose her footing.

Guzzler didn't hesitate. He grabbed her coat in his teeth and pulled back, and the wonder of it was that she didn't shrink away from him but fell instead on the ground towards him as he kept dragging her uphill, back and away from the new cliff that was creating itself before their eyes, leaving the wire and wood of the barrier to sag above the grey sea, with nothing below it now but air and wind, and seagulls wheeling and calling.

And then Miss Grey was shouting to everyone to stay on the far side of the path, running towards where Agatha and Guzzler were and telling Agatha to stay lying down, to crawl forwards with Guzzler. Miss Grey was carefully – not frantically, but quickly – going as close as she dared and then kneeling and pulling Agatha by the hands over the untrustworthy ground until they reached a patch of granite that was firmly embedded, that would surely not move for another thousand years. And then the three of them, the girl and the woman and the dog, huddled in an embrace that went on for a long time.

Mr O'Grady and Sister Joseph and Lilac's mum all appeared to come back to life at the same time, and started calling to the children to stand with them, to gather together as if there was safety in numbers. Lilac felt as though any step she took might take her away too, though she was far back from the edge, and the dark brown earth under the grass she was standing on felt just as solid as it always had. She hadn't even noticed that she was clutching Michael's sleeve as if she might be pulled over the edge by some unseen force if she didn't hold onto something. She kept it tight in her grasp as they both walked slowly, shakily, over to the adults. They heard a shout and looked around to see Mrs Kovac, Agatha's mother, hailing them – she had come to join the walk and was only gradually understanding that something had happened to change the mood of the day from excitement to fear. In a while they would all have moved from fear to relief, and then back to slightly hysterical excitement again, but just now they were still in shock.

Miss Grey, Guzzler and Agatha stood up and moved to join the large group, Agatha finding her mother and melting against her side while Miss Grey explained what had happened.

'Now,' Miss Grey said decisively, even though her voice still held a slight tremor. Everyone listened. 'Sister Joseph can take the rest of the group on; there's no reason not to finish the walk, we have all that money to raise. You can walk on the inland side of the path, you don't have to be afraid of it. It's solid rock underfoot there. You need to tell anyone you meet on the way that it's not safe up here.

'Mrs Kovac and I will walk Agatha down the quick way because we've all had a shock and need to sit down somewhere warm. 'Mrs McGrath,' she looked at Lilac's mother, 'could we go with you to your house? I know it's not far.' Lilac's mother nodded, happy to help. 'And Mr O'Grady, can you walk as fast as possible to make a phone call from the hotel at the end of the strand – I think that's the closest place – and let the Guards know that the path needs to be closed off up here until they can resite the fence safely, and stay till they arrive to stop anyone else coming up?' Mr O'Grady set off at a gallop.

Slowly, Agatha looked down at her hand and unclenched her fist. In it was the curled and yellowing piece of paper she'd been reaching for when she overbalanced – somehow she had managed to grab it as she fell. She held it out towards Lilac. Lilac took it and read the words: 'IRISH HOSPITALS' SWEEPSTAKES TICKET', it said in big letters. 'This entitles the bearer . . .'

Lilac looked up at Agatha and tried to supress the

hysterical giggle that was forming in her throat. 'A sweepstakes ticket? The missing one from the Aquarium? Do you think . . . ?' She turned it over and saw the words 'City Aquarium' scribbled on the back.

'Agatha! You found it!'

Agatha nodded, smiling. She was still beyond words, but her eyes had lost the terrified look they'd held for the past few minutes.

*****

'I think Agatha might be over her fear of dogs,' Nuala said later, as they told Gerry all about the morning. 'She held on tight to Guzzler all the way home. Poor child, such a shock. A cup of hot chocolate did her the world of good, mind you, and Miss Grey let her off school for the rest of the day. Maybe you can invite her over to play during the Christmas holidays, Lilac. She and Guzzler can have a reunion.'

'That would be nice,' Lilac agreed. Maybe it wouldn't have to be just her and Guzzler all the way till Margery came home after all. It was a happy thought. They could even have Jenny O'Herlihy over too, maybe. If she wasn't scared of dogs.

There was a new letter from Margery. It seemed a long time since Margery had left, and a lot had happened. It was hard to imagine that there was still half a year to go before she'd be back, because so much more would have happened by then. Sometimes Lilac could hardly get hold of any feeling of Margery-ness at all, but then when a letter came in the post she could hear Margery's voice saying the words and it was much better than looking at their blurry last-year's class photo and wondering what they'd be doing if she was still here.

Dear Lilac,

Caroline has a new boyfriend. She's really happy now and it's so much nicer with no slamming doors and playing The Cure all the time. She says she and Danny had sworn eternal love but he never wrote, at least only once, so she thinks it wasn't true love after all. She says she's grown as a person and she's getting Dad to take a photo of her with Jean-Claude and she's going to post it to her friends from school at home so that everyone will know she really does have a boyfriend. Oh, wait, I found out l'espion means lezzer. I think it's French for it. Jean-Claude is quite handsome, and has floppy hair that falls over his eyes. He's nice to me, too, he bought me a hot chocolate at the hockey game. That was so that I wouldn't tell Mum that I'd seen him and Caroline kissing pashonatly in the phone booth when she was meant to be gone to the rest room. His hands were under her jacket. But I think he still had his mittens on, because it's cold at the ice rink.

The rest room is what they call the loo here, which is silly because you don't rest there. The first time I heard it I thought it was going to be a nice room with sofas and tellys, but it was just the toilets. I thought people got to go and lie down if they were tired at school, and I was wondering why they always came back so quickly. I thought they were having really quick naps. Then one day I was really tired and I asked if I could go to the rest room but I couldn't find it so I just had to go back to class. Then I thought maybe nobody else could find it either and that's why they came back so soon.

So the moral of the story is that if you need to go to the loo, you ask if you can go to the bathroom and then everyone knows what you mean. Except that there's still no bath in the bathrooms at school.

Love from Margery

Lilac thought about how tricky words were, meaning different things in different places, even in the same language. And she thought about how some answers turned up if you stayed quiet for a while, but other times you had to go and find what you wanted to know by asking straight out. She decided this was one of the asking times.

So she went downstairs again to where her mum was stirring something on the hob.

'What's a lesbian, Mum?'

'A woman who has a girlfriend instead of a boyfriend. Like Aunty Dolly, you know, with Fiona.'

'Oh. I like Fiona. She tells good jokes.'

'Yep. I like her too.'

'But then that's not a bad thing.'

'No. No, it's not.'

A minute passed.

'What's for dinner?'

'Fish fingers. Dad and I are having curry but I know you don't like it.'

'Yum. I'm going to do my homework. I have my last ever spelling test of this year tomorrow.'

'Well, let me know if you need help going over your words.'

'OK.'

CHAPTER 28

Dear Margery,

The sign in the penguin habitat was wrong. It was supposed to say Humboldt Penguins instead of humble penguins. They're a type of penguin that lives further north than the Antarctic, in rocky, sandy areas. The penguins in the Aquarium were fine the whole time.

We went to see the ski slope, because Mum wondered if lessons might be fun, and it turns out that the artificial snow isn't snow at all. It's more like hundreds of scrubbing brushes sticking up and stuck together to make mats that they put down the hill. The penguins wouldn't have liked it.

The Aquarium unbarred me and Agatha after Agatha found the winning sweeps ticket, because it was way more than the concert money and now all their troubles are over. And they said the mistake with the sign was their fault and they'll make sure they double check all the signs in future. But they did say we should ask a grown-up before we take matters into our own hands again. They had to say that, I suppose.

Still, I feel like we won.
Happy Christmas.
Love from Lilac

Dear Miss McCarthy,

Thank you for your recent letter. Here at Greenpeace Headquarters we were sorry to hear about the situation with the penguins in your local aquarium. We are unable to free up resources to work on this just now, but suggest that you gather signatures for a petition, engage your local media outlets (television, radio, newspapers), and/or write to your local elected representative to increase awareness.

Perhaps you could organize a sponsored walk.

We look forward to hearing more about your campaign and wish you every success with it.

Yours sincerely,
John Hunter,
Greenpeace (Ireland).

P.S. This isn't the same aquarium that was just in the news because of the runaway priest, is it?

ACKNOWLEDGMENTS

I have to thank a few people, so that's what this part is for. Alice Bradley, who read the story and told me to keep writing. Jennifer Thorson and Emily Rainsford Ryan, who read early drafts and were kind, but not too kind. My very excellent beta readers Rachel Gribbon, Ciara Hadley, Caer Lavelle, Millie McCarthy, Ella McGrath, and Caoimhe Naessens. Cera Grier, Emily Rainsford Ryan (again) and Suzy Hastings for the cover art and design. And finally B, as always, for ever, for knowing when to say something and when to keep quiet, and my children, who are going to do extraordinary things in the big wide world all too soon.

ABOUT THE AUTHOR

Christine Doran grew up in Dublin, Ireland. At the age of twenty-nine and a half she moved to the United States, where she now lives with her family. *Lilac in Black and White* is her first novel.

To find out more about Lilac's world and to keep up to date with her further adventures, go to

www.lilacthegirl.blogspot.com

Lilac will return in *Lilac in Scarlet*,
coming soon.

CPSIA information can be obtained
at www.ICGtesting.com
Printed in the USA
LVHW081331031021
699374LV00010B/1326